Love's New Beginnings

Julie
I value your
friendship so much
Thanks for being such
a great friend!
love
Diana

Also by Diana Stout

Grendel's Mother
Determined Hearts
Shattered Dreams: A Laurel Ridge Novella (#1)
David & Goliath
"Maggie's Story"
The Super Simple Easy Basic Cookbook
Tomorrow's Wish for Love
Love's New Beginnings

Love's New Beginnings

Diana Stout

Cover design by Sharpened Pencils Productions LLC
Diana Fox (Avalon Books) edition 1996

ISBN: 978-0-9974223-5-1

DEDICATION

To the experience of love and romance in all its finest, from its beginning to its final ending.

CONTENTS

LOVE'S NEW BEGINNINGS

Prologue

His patience had finally paid off.

He watched from across the street as she got out of the cab parked in front of her brownstone, the cabbie opening the trunk pulling out two suitcases. From the backseat, she retrieved a shoulder bag, a purse, dry-cleaning, and what looked like a bag of groceries.

She looked around. It was late. Really late. Like two in the morning late, but he'd been expecting her.

The driver tipped and gone, she now struggled to carry everything in one trip.

Excellent. This was going to be easier than he thought.

Casually, he pushed away from the lamppost, his gaze fastened on her. He needed just one more robbery and he'd be accepted in the gang. Just one more watch or diamond ring.

While other gang members chose more common streets for their victims, he knew this neighbor. He lived a couple streets over, but he knew this neighborhood. Upon until now, he'd been able to perform his robberies when people were working or traveling, but he'd made too many hits and now the neighborhood watch was on alert.

He knew her schedule, thanks to her neighbor, Mike, who was his uncle and with whom he had stayed often enough to meet everyone in the building. No one suspected him and he wanted it left that way. The only thing he was after was her expensive watch, the one she always wore and had shown him and his uncle. A gift from someone close. He already knew she didn't wear any other jewelry, so there was no use looking for more.

He watched as she hoisted the shoulder bag up on her shoulder, and tucked the smaller suitcase under her arm, the plastic bag of groceries hanging from her hand.

He crossed the street, his steps speeding up.

The dry cleaning folded over her arm, she picked up the remaining suitcase.

He broke into a run.

She dropped the suitcase.

He growled, adrenaline feeding him strength.

She bent at the waist.

He rammed into her with everything he had, grabbing at her left arm, twisting the expensive watch off her arm, as she pitched forward. Hearing a sickening thud sounding as her head hit the cement casing, a crack as her left shoulder and arm jammed

10

into the cement steps, he took off running.

Immediately, she was unconscious never knowing what hit her.

Sheets of music, slid out of the shoulder bag, fluttered in the breeze, then scattered down the street. Milk flowed down a step and mingled with scattered oranges.

As he ran, he felt a second's worth of guilt that she'd gotten injured but brushed it aside.

No one would ever know, and tonight, there'd be a celebration as he became the newest member of the gang that thrived on small-time but profitable robberies.

Chapter 1

She could kill for two aspirins right now — one for the pain in her left arm, the other for her head.

"Charlene Walker?"

Her head snapped up. She stifled the urge to groan at the shooting pain. She squinted at a slim, attractive attorney not much older than her own twenty-nine years.

He stuck out his hand. "I'm Aaron Reading. A fan of yours. I heard you were going to be here. Sorry about your grandfather."

Charlene could only nod. Without thinking she slipped her hand in his and winced at the firmness of his handshake. Even though her left arm was in a cast, her right hand and arm were still bruised and sore. He didn't appear to notice her pain. "Thank you," she said, her voice barely above a whisper. She cleared her throat. "It's nice to meet you." Though she would have preferred to be left alone, Charlene knew from past experience to never turn away from a fan.

Another attorney, this one older and balding approached them. She wanted to groan. Would the reading ever get started?

He spoke to the younger man. "Mrs. Wilson is on the phone, wanting to add another codicil to her Will. I told her you'd take care it."

"Yes, sir."

Turning to her, the older man said, "I'm Henry Norton, your grandfather's attorney." She squinted at him. His round face and large oval glasses reminded her of an owl. "Are you all right, my dear?"

She blinked. "Actually, I have a bit of a headache. Could I have some aspirin, please?"

"Of course, my dear." Norton motioned to his secretary.

Charlene massaged her temple, wishing she was finally at Gramps' house where she could relax. Since the mugging, headaches were a daily occurrence anytime she felt stressed. Between not getting into Willow Junction until midnight, trying to find a motel, listening to her birds' incessant chatter, not sleeping well, her throbbing arm, and now this throbbing headache, she felt lousy. Drained actually. The stress was overwhelming.

"Here we go." He pressed two aspirins into her palm. "Let's go into my office." To his secretary he said, "Buzz me when he gets here."

Norton led her to his office. She settled into one of a pair of burgundy leather upholstered chairs in front of the desk and accepted a glass of water. Tossing the aspirin into her mouth, she swallowed them down, then set the glass on the corner of his massive oak desk. "Thank you."

"So sorry to hear you'd been mugged. Crime is out of control in the big cities these days."

His buzzer sounded. He picked up the phone. "Send him in," Norton said, into his phone. Immediately, the door opened. To Charlene, he said, "Here's Logan now."

Charlene couldn't get up if she wanted to. The chair was too comfortable and she didn't have the energy. Charlene was surprised that anyone else would be at the reading of her grandfather's Will. But then, when she thought about it, she really didn't know the details of his life.

Hearing a deep rumbling voice, her curiosity got the best of her. She peered around the chair but he was already so close, she had to look up. The bluest eyes she had ever seen stared at her, his gaze pinning her to the chair. They reminded her of the sky on a clear summer's day. A memory tugged at her. Dismissing it, she extended her hand automatically as Norton introduced her.

"Nice to meet you." The deep base timbre of his voice was a soothing sound to her ears. His large hand engulfed hers. Immediately, she felt his warmth. Despite his strength and that his hand was twice as large as hers, he held her hand gently. She could feel callouses across his palm.

He towered over her like a Sequoia. At five-two everyone was taller than she, but Logan was easily more than six-foot, she estimated. His hair was blond and he looked wickedly handsome in his sports jacket sans tie. The top two buttons of his shirt were undone, revealing bronzed skin. Charlene wondered if his entire chest was just as bronzed.

"I'm sorry about your grandfather," Logan said. "He was a nice man."

She looked up again. For the second time, she was spellbound by the brilliance of blue and a memory she couldn't pinpoint. "Thank you."

Norton sat, indicating for Logan to sit also.

As Logan circled her chair, Charlene thought she smelled chocolate and cherry—a deadly, but rich combination. If she had any weakness, it was chocolate covered cherries.

Logan's shirt buttons strained at their openings as he eased into the chair. He extended his long legs out in front of him and crossed them at the ankles.

Though she couldn't name it, the atmosphere in the room had changed. It was charged now, and she sensed the source was Logan.

"With your permission, Charlene, rather than reading the entire Will and boring you both, let me explain the terms as simply as I can."

"Please." She couldn't have endured listening to a tedious reading of thee and thou, whatsoever and whosoever.

"Your grandfather's terms aren't simple, but they're easy to understand. What Charlie did was this—you and Logan have each inherited one half of the orchard and its business, a hundred acres total, fifty each."

Charlene was dumbfounded. She had no idea who this Logan Taylor was, but certainly he didn't deserve half her grandfather's livelihood.

Her heart racing, she peeked a glance at Logan. He sat stone-like, not one emotion displayed on his face, his gaze focused on the attorney.

"Charlene," Norton continued. She turned her gaze back to the attorney. "You've inherited the rest of Charlie's assets, chiefly the house, its contents, and his cash holdings. About five hundred dollars in a savings account.

"Now here's where it starts to get complicated. Charlie's Will stipulates that neither of you can sell the orchard to an outsider."

"That's ridiculous!" Charlene burst out. She glanced at Logan again. Still no reaction. She frowned. How could Gramps have done this to her?

Norton continued. "You can only sell to each other. And only after a year's time."

"A year?" She couldn't stand it. She jumped up from her chair, instantly regretting the sharp jolt to her head, but now she had more problems than a mere headache. A hand to her aching head, she paced to the door and back to her chair. Standing behind it, she rested her broken arm on the back of the chair and gripped the leather with her other hand. "It's ridiculous. None of this makes any sense."

All her plans—

No, she couldn't think about anything else right now. Take it easy, she told herself. Listen to Norton. He's not done yet. Maybe he's got some good news. She moved around to the front of the chair and sat down again. "Sorry. This is just so unexpected. Makes no sense at all."

Norton continued. "Unfortunately, it made sense to Charlie. There's more. Neither of you can make any changes to the orchard nor its operation without permission of your partner."

"Explain to me how this makes sense?" Charlene demanded.

"Your grandfather knew Logan was interested in owning the orchard and if Charlie had had no family, he would have given Logan the entire property."

Norton addressed Logan. "Charlie fully appreciated your hard work and realized during these last years you were responsible for the orchard's success."

"You worked for Gramps?" she asked, looking at him and not caring that she was frowning.

He looked at her, his gaze steady. "Yes."

Norton spoke again, this time to her. "Your grandfather always believed in family. He believed the orchard should remain in the family. He knew you felt the same way."

Charlene felt guilty. She might have felt that way earlier, before the accident. Before the mess that had become her life. She had come to Willow Junction prepared to sell her grandfather's property—everything—to the highest bidder.

"As to the house," Norton continued.

Charlene closed her eyes, shuddering at what stipulations might be attached to it. Opening her eyes, she prepared for the worst.

"You've inherited it, providing you live in it, starting now, for the next six months. If you return to New York during that time, you forfeit your inheritance to the house and its contents. The house will be sold, along with the contents, with the money going back into the business. The cash, the five hundred dollars, remains yours regardless of what you do. After six months, you can choose to sell the house or keep it."

Charlene sank back against the chair. Unbelievable. Totally unbelievable. This would be the straw that broke her financial camel's back. "Isn't there any way around this? I've got to get back to New York. My condo—"

"Not unless you want to lose the house."

"Do you know why he did this?" she asked. "I mean, other than the reasons you've already stated?"

"Yes, but I can't reveal that information. Believe me when I say I tried to talk your grandfather out of this. He was one stubborn man."

"Like a mule," Logan murmured.

Norton handed her a manila envelope.

"What's this?"

"Charlie's bank book, checkbook, important documents, the keys to his truck, keys to the house—I didn't even think. Where did you stay last night? You could have stayed at the house."

"It was late when I got in. I stayed at a motel."

"Do either of you have any other questions?"

At the moment, she had none. She was too stunned to think. Logan didn't say anything, so apparently, he didn't have any questions either.

19

"Well, then. If anything comes up that needs my attention, you know where to reach me."

Charlene waited until Logan left, shutting the door behind him. "Mr. Norton—"

"Please, call me Henry."

"Henry. What can you tell me about Logan Taylor?"

"If you're worried about having him as a partner, don't. He's hardworking, a solid citizen. He's a man you can trust, someone you want on your side."

Charlene frowned. Trust. She didn't have much left these days for anyone, no matter how highly recommended they came. There was something about Logan that was unsettling, and if there was anything she'd learned lately, it was to trust her instincts.

* * * * *

Out on the sidewalk, Logan waited for her.

Once she spotted him, he saw her hesitate. Charlene Walker, world-renown pianist, looked just like her publicity photos. Picture perfect. The forest green silk suit hugged her lush curves, the breeze ruffling the smooth material tight against those curves, the skirt hugging her thighs. Earlier, it'd been difficult keeping his gaze on Norton when he'd rather watch her skirt creep up her thigh. He was both relieved and crushed when she had jumped up, those legs no longer tantalizing him. Now a strand of brown hair had escaped the confines of the bun at the nape of her neck that was her signature hairdo. Every picture Charlie had ever shown him and those he saw on the covers of magazines, she always had that bun.

He wondered what her hair looked like down.

Coming out of the door and coming down the steps, she looked frail, her hand clasping the handrail in a death grip. For just an instant, he considered stepping forward and helping her.

Then he saw her lift her chin and straighten her spine, a purposeful look in her brown eyes.

He didn't want to care one hoot about this woman even if she was his partner. The first chance he had, he was buying her out. Yet, there was something about her that attracted him. He couldn't stop watching her. He felt like an over-stretched rubber band, the tension he felt inside so taut, he thought he'd snap.

With precision and grace unlike anything he'd seen before, she walked toward him, then stopped. She had to. He blocked the sidewalk.

He looked down at her. No bigger than a child, he thought, slight and obviously tired, but she looked ready to do battle. "We have to talk," he said.

"I agree," she replied. "I want to know your intentions, your plans, and what kind of influence you had over Gramps."

Logan squinted his eyes. Of all the raw, rotten—

"Right now isn't a good time. I've got to be out of the motel by noon, and it's—," Charlene glanced at her watch. "—nearly that already. The boys are going to chew me out for leaving them alone that long. Can you meet me at Gramps' house, say in two hours? It's the best I can offer."

"Fine. I've got some repairs to finish anyway." He knew he sounded waspish, but at this moment, he didn't care. He could be just as short but polite with her as she was with him.

"Good. I'll see you then." She started to move forward, but couldn't. "Excuse me."

Forced to step aside, he stared after her. Darn, if she wasn't great to look at as she walked away. He should be riled at the high-handed way she had accused him of manipulating Charlie. Fortunately, he'd had lots of practice thanks to Charlie—and Beth—on how to control his temper and how to bide his time. Charlene didn't know it yet, but she was just like the old man. Logan knew how to handle her. There was plenty of time to straighten things out. Straighten her out, too, if he had anything to say about it.

* * * * *

Weary from the week's total events, Charlene opened the door of the fire-engine red Mustang she'd rented last night at the airport. It had been that or a Cadillac. Behind the wheel, she jammed the keys into the ignition. Looking up, Logan stood at the side of a dusty two-tone blue pickup watching her. If anything, his scowl had deepened.

The wind tousled his hair and ruffled the papers in his hand. He stood with his feet in a wide stance, standing as if he owned the ground he stood on. Even from this distance, she could feel the intensity of his cobalt blue eyes as they bore into her. Though it was over one-hundred degrees in the shut-up car, Charlene felt goosebumps break out on her arms as if the temperature was freezing instead.

Without taking her gaze off Logan, she quickly turned over

the ignition. It caught and she punched the air-conditioner on. Immediately, cool air caressed her all too warm face.

Just what I need, she thought. A partner with an attitude.

Realizing, she was wasting precious minutes, Charlene shifted into gear and tried as best she could with her broken arm to swing into traffic.

As she drove past Logan, she tried not to look his way. She couldn't help herself. She looked. She shivered at the look he gave her. What had Gramps done to her?

* * * * *

"Your place or mine?"

"Kiss me, baby."

"All right, you two," Charlene said to her companions. She turned the steering wheel one-handed, guiding the rental car past the apple orchard. She noticed the trees were heavy with ripening fruit. Good. She desperately needed the orchard to do well. Once she'd passed the orchard, she turned down the lane that led to Gramps' house. Her house now. "We're almost there. Do you think you can hold it down?"

"Not in this lifetime, Toots," the African gray parrot chirped, perched on the headrest of the passenger seat. He'd made such a fuss being in his cage, she had let him out so he could look out the windows. Thankfully, he'd been content to sit there the entire drive.

"I want a kiss," the large macaw demanded. He sat in his cage, the door open, content to remain on the swing as it moved with the motion of the car.

In her condo, she left their cage doors open when she was home, so they were used to having some freedom.

After the long flight to Detroit yesterday, the two-hour drive to Willow Junction, a small village northeast of Marshall near Duck Lake, and having to leave the birds in their cages at the motel for fear one of the maids would unwittingly let them out the front door when she came in to clean while Charlene was out, she had been reluctant to confine them to their cages during the drive out here. She probably should have left them at home, but after her hospital stay, she had to admit she missed their stupid banter. Plus, Mike, her neighbor, friend, and the first-chair violinist with the New York Symphony where they had first met, wasn't able to watch the boys when she had left to come here. Now, considering she'd be here for six months, she was glad she had brought them. At the moment though, she could do without their usual exclamations.

"Can't you guys be good for just a few minutes?"

"I'll be good." This from the macaw.

"Thanks, Stan. Now if we can convince your friend Ollie —"

"Speech, speech!" Ollie cried.

Ignoring their chatter, Charlene concentrated on easing the car to a stop in the shadow of the large rambling farmhouse. At one time, the yard had held magnificent gardens. Now, there were only weeds and huge lilac bushes almost reaching second-story height. The house appeared shabbier and more rundown than she remembered. A coat of paint would brighten the house up. Unfortunately, she wouldn't be doing it. Someone else would have to spruce it up.

On the way back to the motel earlier, Charlene had made her first decision. She was going to sell the house. With Gramps gone, she had no other family. She certainly didn't want to live here. Her life was in New York. It didn't make sense to keep the house unless she wanted to rent it and that didn't appeal to her either. She needed the money more than she needed to keep his memory alive. It saddened her that she didn't have a choice in the matter.

The birds ruffled their feathers. They were getting restless.

"Okay, guys. We're here. Ollie, get in Stan's cage."

"Oh, no!" Stan cried.

"It's just for a few minutes," she promised him. "With my broken arm I can only carry one cage at a time. Listen to me," she mumbled to herself. "I'm talking to two dumb birds."

"I'm home," Ollie said, hopping into Stan's cage.

"Oh, no!" Stan repeated.

Charlene turned off the ignition. Before she opened the back door, she made sure Ollie was in the cage as he'd pronounced. Shutting the cage door, she lifted the cage from the seat, which had been protected with a towel.

Charlene gazed at the house as she approached it. She wished she could extend the driveway around to the front of the house, making it a circle drive, rather than parking the car here on the side, where there was no door, just well-worn grass where a car had always been parked. She remembered Gramps had wanted to make that improvement. It'd be a lot more convenient than

25

having to walk through the grass, toting everything across the yard.

As she rounded the back corner of the house, Stan and Ollie resumed their chatter. Now they played their favorite game. Cops and robbers.

"Hands above your head!" Stan said.

"Spread 'em!" Ollie returned.

"They're up and I'm spread!"

Charlene's head snapped up at the sound of a male voice.

Chapter 2

"All I've got is twenty bucks. It's yours if you want it."

In front of her stood a man with his back to her, his hands up in the air, his long, lean legs spread. Instantly, she recognized Logan; she'd remember that stance anywhere.

A carpenter's belt, holding an assortment of tools, rode low on his hips. He had changed. Softened blue jeans that had been new long ago hugged his behind. A cute behind at that. Her eyes followed the line of his navy, plaid flannel shirt to his broad shoulders and to his arms that were raised in the air.

One hand held a hammer, the other a couple of nails. Rolled-up sleeves revealed blond curling hairs on tanned forearms. His hair was shaggy in the back, in obvious need of a haircut. Funny, she hadn't noticed that in Norton's office.

A broken board and a new plank rested against the porch. A gaping hole where the second step should have been told Charlene he'd been repairing the step.

"Logan, I..." She paused. She giggled.

Slowly, Logan twisted his head and peered at her. His eyes were even more penetrating than they'd been earlier today. She didn't know whether to flee or stay. She watched as he lowered his arms and turned around, his gaze never leaving hers. In his sports jacket, he could have passed for a model. Now, he looked rugged and equally at home in these clothes as he had in his jacket. His chin was square, and there were hollows just beneath his cheekbones. His lips were firm as he studied the lingering yellow bruises on her arms and face.

She squirmed realizing he hadn't seen them earlier because of the long-sleeves. But now, she wore short sleeves that exposed a number of bruises.

"I hope the other guy looks worse," Logan said.

"Shoot him!" one bird squawked.

"Hands above your head!" the other responded.

Charlene's face warmed, but she was grateful for the bird's diversion. She really didn't want to talk about herself right now. "My birds—"

"Want to dance?" Ollie interrupted.

"Enough!" she said to the birds. They ruffled their feathers then sat quietly. "Look, I'm sorry. At times they can be quite a nuisance."

A corner of Logan's mouth quirked. Her heart fluttered at the hint of his smile. He needed to smile more often.

"There hasn't been a crime committed in Willow Junction in over twenty years. I couldn't believe I was going to be the first victim. Here, let me take that cage. It must be heavy."

His fingers brushed hers. Surprised at his touch, she jerked her hand back. Logan's eyebrows lifted at her reaction.

He held out his hand to help her up and over the missing step, and she hesitated. He's only trying to help, she thought chastising herself. Nothing more. It wasn't his fault she was so skittish lately. She put her hand in his, instantly aware again of his hard-callused skin against her softer palm.

He opened the screen door. She paused again. She felt uneasy having a stranger following her into her home, but there was absolutely nothing to be afraid of here, she reminded herself. Willow Junction was a small community of only two hundred fifty people.

"I'm not going to hurt you."

"I didn't say you were. Or would."

"Your actions and your eyes said otherwise. They're large and quite expressive, you know. And very brown. Just like a doe's. You don't trust me, do you?"

"In a word, no."

"Charlie knew me and trusted me for seventeen years."

"But I'm not Charlie. Some things can't be inherited or passed on." She sighed. "It isn't just you. Right now, I don't trust anyone."

Following him inside, she quickly became absorbed in the house. She walked the long hall that ran the entire length of the house, ending at the front door. In summer, with both doors open, she remembered the circulation created was better than any fan.

She glanced around. The house was smaller than she remembered, but that was only natural. She'd grown and memories tended to soften. Seventeen years had passed since she'd been here. She'd been twelve at the time, spending several weeks with her grandfather and getting to know him.

After that, the last time she'd seen him was at her high school graduation. He had come especially for the occasion.

Soon after her career as a concert pianist began in earnest, her mother had died. Gramps had offered her a home, but she already had a home of her own in New York, plus she traveled too much to live elsewhere.

So, she and Gramps wrote, exchanging letters several times a year. She should have suspected something was wrong, however, when he didn't respond to her letters as quickly as he used to. But then, she'd been busy with her ever-growing career and sent him postcards from around the world.

Looking around, nothing had changed really. It was like stepping back in time.

The parlor, as Gramps had called it, was immediately to her right and still crowded with furniture. The well-preserved antiques stood exactly as Gram, who'd died twenty years ago, had arranged the room. Fondly, she remembered how Gramps' face would light up whenever he'd talked about his wife—her father's mother. Charlene had only met her a couple times when she was young, so young that she had no real memory of those visits. Only what her mother had told her.

She ached at the thought that she'd never see Gramps again.

"What a dump!" Ollie said.

Charlene spun around. For a moment, she'd forgotten about Logan and the birds.

Logan held the cage up and peered at the two birds. "Are they like this all the time?"

Her eyes strayed to the muscles in his shoulder and arm that showed little strain, belying the weight of the cage as he held it in the air. "Yes, I'm afraid they are rather talkative. They have the uncanny ability to say the wrong things at just the right time. Here," she said, walking to a table near a window.

As she passed him, she caught a whiff of a musky pine scent, plus a hint of chocolate again. With shaky hands, she removed several small-framed family pictures from the tabletop. "Set the cage here for now." She watched the taut cording of his forearm as he set it gently on the ivory-colored doily, disturbing the birds as little as possible. She laid the pictures on the nearby sofa.

It was then she noticed the piano in the corner. So badly, she wanted to sit down and play. Instead, she listened to the birds chatter to one another and to no one in particular and went through the second archway eager to see the rest of the house. The huge table circled by chairs sat in the dining room just as she remembered. Like the parlor, there was too much furniture in here, but it was easy to picture the huge table, with all its leaves added, extended to accommodate a large family gathered around it for a holiday meal. She imagined a big Thanksgiving turkey being brought from the kitchen. Women squeezing around the chairs as they brought out rolls, potatoes, and pies. A family gathering the likes of which she'd never had.

An only child, her parents divorced when she was young. She never saw her father as he lived in California and wasn't one for phone calls or letters. He never remembered her birthday and after the first year forgot holidays completely. It was always just her and her mother, and as a nurse, her mother usually worked holidays. It meant double-time money, which they needed.

At least, Charlene had been able to show her mother an easier life before she had died.

"How old are they?" Logan asked, following her, interrupting her thoughts.

"The birds? Over forty. Their exact age I don't know. A neighbor received them as a fiftieth wedding anniversary gift. A year ago, she got pneumonia and was hospitalized. She was eighty-nine and never returned to her apartment. Since she had no other family, I kept the birds. At first, Stan and Ollie drove me crazy, but I got used to them. Now, I can't imagine being without them."

"Stan and Ollie?" Logan laughed. "Their names fit."

"They love to mimic movies."

From the parlor they both heard, "Here kitty, kitty. Here kitty, kitty."

Charlene chuckled, just as she always did whenever she heard them calling a cat.

"And obviously, they have a death wish," he added.

"Seems that way," she said, running her hand across the top

of the table. It was oak and would be beautiful once it was stripped of the darkened varnish that made it look worn out and ugly.

Logan watched her fondle the tops of the chairs. Her fingers were long and tapered, her nails short and manicured without polish. She barely touched the wood, her hand skimming over the surface. "I imagine you're eager to get rid of this junk."

"Heavens no." She sighed. "I wish I could keep it all. They're valuable antiques, far from being junk, but I need to sell most of it, refinishing it first. Buyers want to see beyond the discolored varnish and want distressed furniture. My mother used to refinish furniture as a second job. A hobby of hers, actually." She went to the credenza and traced the intricate carving with her finger. He swallowed, watching her hand caress the tall oak legs. Her caress was innocent, yet, oh, so sensual. He wondered what her hands would feel like on him. The picture in his mind heated his skin. He tried to concentrate on her voice instead.

Ever since he first saw her in Norton's office, she'd been on his mind. The stark white cast, a hauntingly pale face would have drawn anyone's attention. Now, she wore expensive khaki pants, a pale-yellow camp shirt, expensive looking loafers with cream-colored silk socks. Certainly not a wardrobe he was used to seeing in Willow Junction. He'd learned enough from Beth as to what was expensive. She'd had champagne tastes on his beer budget. It was Charlene's hands and eyes that interested him most. Even now, the depth of her velvet brown eyes and delicate hands drew him in.

"Most of the furniture needs to be restored, but none of it's damaged," Charlene continued. "That makes it all the more valuable."

"I'd get rid of it all and get something more modern," he said swiftly.

"Do you have any idea how many people want to own furniture like this?"

Logan shook his head.

"They do. I know people in New York who would kill to own pieces like this." *Kills me that I have to sell it all*, she thought. She would have enjoyed restoring the farmhouse and its contents, keeping some of it.

"Why didn't you come to the funeral?" Logan asked.

His question startled her. "You get right to the point, don't you?" In New York... but she wasn't in New York, she thought checking herself. "Gramps always said there was no need for phones in Willow Junction. Just tell your neighbor and before the day was done, everyone would know."

"It's easier that way," he replied. "Getting right to the point is just as important as honesty in my book. Saves lots of time. So, why didn't you come?"

Charlene stared out the window. She bit her lip, wondering how much she should tell him. Logan may have worked for Gramps for years, but to her, he was still a stranger.

"I was out of the country when he died," she said turning to him. "Then I... I was in the hospital."

She watched his gaze follow the bruises on her face, her arms, her neck, and the one on her uninjured hand. Charlene was grateful he couldn't see the rest of her. She decided to test his sincerity about being honest. "I'd rather not talk about it right now."

He studied her, his legs spread, once again in that way that said this was his territory. "Okay, then. Later."

His stance stirred her memory. That and his blue eyes. "You know, you look awfully familiar. Have we met before? If you worked for Gramps, how come I never saw you when I was here or heard about you in his letters?"

His eyes...

And then she remembered. "Wait a minute. That summer I was here there was a tall, skinny kid with no shoulders at the door looking for work. It was pouring rain and he looked like a drowned ra—He was soaked. That was you." He had stared at her then, too.

"Yeah. That was me. You were standing behind Charlie. You were all leg and your knees looked huge." He looked down at her legs. "You've covered them up... your knees." Oh, he remembered all right. Back then, she had the longest legs he'd ever seen on a girl and her knees were dimpled. He'd been a leg man ever since, and she had grown into those legs beautifully. "Nice knees," he commented. Who was he kidding? She had great legs, the best he'd ever seen.

"Nice shoulders," she responded quickly. Lord, what made her blurt that out loud? Never had she spent as much time admiring a man as she was right now. If anything, she should be feeling animosity toward this stranger who had become her partner.

"How come you never came back to visit?"

"It never worked out. After Dad died when I was little, I remember hearing Gramps and Mom fighting. He blamed Mom for taking Dad away from the orchard. Mom never stopped me from talking or seeing Gramps, but I never liked leaving her alone. That one summer, I was here was because she was going back to school, and she had convinced me it'd be better for her if I came here. She talked me into it that summer but never again. I was so lonely. Of course, it could have been my age then, too."

She turned and strolled through the rest of lower floor, acutely aware he continued to follow her.

"What did you do for Gramps?" she asked.

"Everything and anything." He shrugged. "I'm handy with a hammer, so I did repairs and any renovation needed. As we both aged, I did more of the field work, trimming, picking, spraying. At the end, his arthritis prevented him from leaving the house, you know."

Surprised, she turned and faced him. "Arthritis?"

"You never knew?"

"No, he never mentioned it in his letters. When did it start bothering him?"

"Ever since I can remember, but not severely until about a year ago."

"I wonder why he never mentioned it."

"He was a proud man and a tough one."

"And he lived here all alone?"

"Oh, he had no problem moving around. He just moved

36

more slowly, that's all. I checked up on him every day. And I always made sure he ate well."

"I... Thank you. I wish I had known. I wish I could have seen him more."

"Why didn't you?"

She hesitated. "I wasn't in the country much. When I was, I was always performing. How come I never saw you after that one time? Strange that our paths didn't cross more often that summer."

"They did. You just never noticed."

The phone rang. She turned toward the sound remembering the phone—a landline—was downstairs on the kitchen wall, across the hall, and one was upstairs in the master bedroom. Behind her, the front screen door clamored shut and she heard the clatter of Logan's boots as he went down the porch steps.

She moved into the kitchen and picked up and phone.

"Hello?"

Silence. Fear washed over Charlene. It was starting again. She couldn't breathe, she started to shake. "He... hello," she said weakly.

"Sorry," a muffled voice said. "Wrong number."

The line went dead.

Charlene closed her eyes, her body limp with relief. She hung up the receiver.

She'd been wrong. Just a wrong number. She looked at the phone, wondering if she could get a new phone, one with caller I.D. If the calls continued, she would.

About a month before the mugging, she began getting a lot

of phone calls on her cell. No one there, hang-ups, and wrong numbers. Lots of them. She didn't think anything about it until the mugging. Her second one, actually. The first had occurred her first year in New York. The Maestro said the hang-ups were just a coincidence, he'd gotten them, too. Just before coming here, she had changed her cell phone number. Only her agent, the Maestro, and her neighbor Mike had the number.

She looked at the wall phone. This wasn't the same thing at all. This was Gramps' phone, his number. Few people knew she was here. Since that first mugging, she was always checking her locks, looking around, conscious of who was near. She'd gotten sloppy that night, was more tired than usual with Gramps on her mind, thinking about the funeral.

Taking a deep cleansing breath, Charlene went into the hall. Logan stood just inside, filling the door frame, a suitcase in each hand.

"What have you got in here?" he asked. "Bricks?"

"Music books."

He looked at her arm. "Wishful thinking?"

"No. I won't be in this cast forever. I'll need to practice."

"But you didn't know you were going to be here for six months."

"I never travel without my music. I'd rather forget a toothbrush than leave home without the music."

A scratching sound came from the door.

"What's that?" she asked.

Logan opened the door. The ugliest calico cat Charlene had

38

ever seen padded in, first rubbing up against Logan's leg, then her own.

"This is—"

"Cat. I remember Cat," she said excitedly. "He was a stray when Gramps rescued him, that summer I was here. The wettest skinniest kitten I'd ever seen. I remember wanting Cat to sleep with me, but he always chose Gramps."

"Yeah, they were a pair, those two. You rarely saw one without the other."

Cat weaved in and out and around Charlene's legs.

"I think he's adopted you already. I'm surprised. He doesn't react to strangers very well."

She noticed the animal walked funny, almost lopsided. "What's wrong with him?"

"He's got arthritis, plus he's blind in one eye. In cat years, he's in the sunset of his life."

"Why didn't Gramps put him to sleep? He's got to be in pain."

"I guess they were a comfort to each other. But, he's not in pain according to the vet."

"You had him checked out?"

"Yes, because I thought the same as you, that he was in pain."

"What will happen to him when I sell the house?"

"Guess you could take him to the Humane Society."

"No one would adopt him. He's too old."

"Take him back to New York."

"I can't do that either. Pets aren't allowed in the building."

"You've got the birds."

"They're an exception. Why don't you take him?"

"It wouldn't work. Cat refuses to live anywhere but here. I took Cat home with me when Charlie died, but he keeps coming back here. We just came over here every day to take care of him."

We. Logan had said we. Charlene blinked. She hadn't even considered that Logan might have a wife. Stupid to think he'd still be single at his age.

It didn't matter. The last thing she needed or wanted was another relationship. She was still recovering from the last one. Such as it was. Or, as she thought it had been, she corrected.

Just then the birds started calling kitty again.

"Oh, oh," she said, seeing Cat turn his head toward the room. He padded into the parlor, and she and Logan looked at each other. "Do you think Stan and Ollie will be all right?"

"Only time will tell. Have you got a stand for that thing?" he asked, indicating the cage.

"No. In New York, they each have a large cage. These cages I brought with me, I use for travel. Thankfully, the Maestro, my mentor, was able to get me on a private plan for this trip—all of them actually, whenever I had to take the birds. I do need to put Ollie into his own cage, though."

"I'll get it." He disappeared into the hall. She heard the screen door slam. A minute later he returned with the cage. "Where do you want it?"

"Next to Stan's cage. Even though they like to keep each

other company, they don't do well living together," she said.

"Like some people," Charlene heard him mutter.

Quickly, she moved Ollie out of Stan's cage and into his own. Cat, with his tail twitching, sat on the floor near Charlene's feet, watching the whole procedure with feline interest.

Finished, Charlene stepped away to watch what Cat would do. Instantly, he was up on the table, demonstrating he had some agility left and seated himself between the two cages, his head twisting back and forth as the birds chattered to each other. Stan, observing Cat, decided he wanted a closer look and hopped down from his high swing to a lower bar and then scooted to the wall of his cage. Cat, at that moment, decided he wanted to get closer, too, and stuck his paw in the cage.

Stan bit it. Cat howled, withdrew his paw, shook it, then jumped off the table. Once on the floor, he sat, looking back up at the cages. The birds started their kitty calling again.

With a final twitch of his tail, Cat turned his back on them and padded out of the room.

"I guess Stan and Ollie are safe enough," she laughed.

"Yeah, looks like the birds have the advantage."

The phone rang again. Asking where she wanted her suitcases, she told him to leave them in the upstairs hall. He went up the stairs, taking them two at a time as she went to the kitchen to answer the phone.

Nervously, she picked up the handset. It was the Maestro. She had forgotten she'd given him Gramps' telephone number.

"Maestro. I was going to call you."

"You arrived safely then."

"Yes. I've got bad news."

"No, Charlene. This is too much for you. First—"

"No, No, Maestro," she said, interrupting him. She didn't want a recounting of her recent losses. Especially of Robert. "It's not *that* kind of bad news. Gramps' Will was read today. For reasons too complicated to explain right now, I've got to stay here for six months."

"Six months!" For a moment, neither of them said anything. Then the Maestro said, "Ah, maybe it's just as well. Less frustration while your arm heals."

On one hand, the Maestro was right; if she was back in New York she'd be driving everyone crazy, wanting to practice but unable to. It was only natural she wanted to spend time doing what she loved most.

Ever since joining the New York Philharmonic Orchestra when she was seventeen, the Maestro had taken her under his wing. He agreed with her teachers that her talent was rare for someone so young. Then, when she'd gone on her first tour as a concert pianist when she was eighteen, he'd taken a leave of absence from his duties as conductor. Her mother couldn't leave her job, and Charlene was just earning enough so they didn't have to eat macaroni and cheese every night. Joining her, the Maestro had jeopardized his job. She never knew that until much later. For a year, he escorted and chaperoned her from country to country. His son, David, who was a few years older than she and an accomplished musician getting a foothold in the country music industry, had accompanied them for a month, acting as their general manager, seeing to all the necessary details that cropped up from day to day. Unfortunately, he had to leave her tour to deal with his own career.

When they returned to the states, she was a star, and the Maestro became America's favorite conductor. Ever since, David and his father became her family, more so after her mother died a year later.

"Just call me now and then," the Maestro continued. "Let me know that you're fine."

"I'll be okay," she said automatically.

"I know you will. You've survived more in your life already than most do in a lifetime. I just want you to be safe."

"I promise I won't be doing anything more here than watching the leaves turn color." Tears came to her eyes. "Say goodbye to everyone for me. I'll miss them."

Charlene hung up the phone. She looked down at the heavy cast on her arm. Her world had been blown apart the night she'd broken her arm, and despite what all the doctors had said, she was determined to put it back together.

Charlene heard pounding. Assuming Logan was back at work on the porch, she went outside, the screen door shutting and latching behind her. Logan was putting away his tools. A butterfly drifted across the repaired steps. The droning hum of bees mingling among the mums that surrounded the porch sounded pleasant to her ears. Charlene watched as Logan slid the hammer into his tool belt, the handle resting against his thigh.

She bit her lip and looked out across the bit of orchard that was near the house. She didn't like how she was attracted to him. He was a married man.

"Thanks for fixing the step," she said.

"No problem. I promised Charlie I would. I'll come back and check the furnace and chimney. The evenings are already cooling down."

Charlene prickled. He wasn't even asking. Just telling her he was going to do it.

"If you're planning on selling the house," he continued, "it would make sense to have everything working properly."

He had a point. It was stupid to get possessive about the property. It wouldn't be hers for long. "You're right. Thank you."

"If there's anything you need while you're here, just give me a call. I live next door." He pointed to a line of hedges at the edge of the back yard. "My house is on the other side of them."

Charlene looked toward the direction Logan indicated. Gramps' total yard was several acres with the house centered on the land. Next door wasn't all that close but close enough if she needed anything. It would be hard getting used to this much space. She was used to being surrounded by people whenever she was in New York. Even in her brownstone, there were people on either side of her, below and above her.

Suddenly, Logan was reluctant to leave. And, he didn't know why. He wondered how she'd cope in her frail condition. Stop kidding yourself, he thought. She's from New York. She had to be one tough cookie. But, she didn't look tough. She had more bruises than a boxer even on his worst day. Nor did she act tough. She seemed hesitant, looking more like a lost soul than an internationally-known celebrity. He added, "There's a convenience store with gas pumps on Main Street where you can get a few groceries and supplies to tide you over."

"I think I passed it on my way here."

Logan glanced at his watch. "But they're probably closed by now."

Silently cursing himself and knowing he was courting trouble, he couldn't stop himself from asking. "There's a truck stop down the road. Nothing fancy, but it has good food. Do you want to get a hamburger?"

She hesitated. "What about your wife?"

"I don't have one." Silently, he cursed. He'd nearly growled it out. If he were smart, he'd speak up, stating he had changed his mind, that he had an appointment or something. But, he didn't.

Again, she hesitated. Finally, she said, "I am hungry."

"You might want your jacket. The weather changes fast. Besides, the sun will be gone by the time we get back. Though it's just September, the nights are cool. Okay if I use your phone?"

"Sure, go ahead."

As Logan walked through the house and into the kitchen, he swore softly. Now, why had he gone and done that, asking her out? She looked resourceful enough. As he went to the phone, he knew she could have found a can of soup or something in Charlie's cupboards. It was pure foolishness for him to get involved with this woman. She'd be nothing but trouble, which meant he had to double down on his goal in getting the orchard from her. Whatever the costs.

After he made his call home, he went to the hall to wait. Despite all the reasons why he shouldn't have asked her out, Logan was also glad he had. He didn't get out much. Though, if the truth were known, it was Charlene herself that made him invite her out. Something about her that drew him to her. He had expected Charlie's granddaughter to have a big city attitude — *here I am you lucky people*. It had surprised him that she didn't, especially considering her celebrity status. Charlie had bragged about her accomplishments every time he got a letter from her. Logan wished now he had listened more carefully.

Minutes later, he watched as she descended the stairs, her small hand hugging the rail. She'd freshened her lipstick; the apple rose color a bright spot on her otherwise pale face. Her photos had always revealed a beautiful woman at the piano, but as she walked toward him, Logan realized the photos didn't do her justice.

Just seconds ago, he had silently spouted his desire to stay away from her, but as she approached him her eyes was his undoing. They were incredible. A velvety brown that shimmered like silk, making his mind and his will as soft as butter every time she looked up at him. And now, that she stood just in front of him, he noted her lips were full. Luscious. Beckoning. Kissable.

"I'm ready."

So was he.

She looked up at him.

He wanted to destroy the thing or kill the person who had

caused her bruises. In time, the bruises would disappear, but would he ever be able to forget how frail she looked at this moment?

A bulky cream-colored sweater was draped over her cast. He took it from her and with Charlene still facing him, he stretched his arms out, opening the sweater behind her, then sheathing her shoulders. His hands remained on her shoulders.

Chapter 3

They stared at each other for a long moment. With every muscle he had, Logan resisted leaning toward her. Her eyes widened even more. She licked her lips. His heart pounded and he silently cursed.

He swallowed, his voice coming out as a rasp. "Shall we go?"

She shivered.

He pulled the top edges of the sweater's front together, attempting to cover her broken arm. "Cold?"

"Nn... just a little."

With a hand at her back, Logan led her out the door and tucked her into his pickup. Closing her door, he walked around the back of the vehicle slowly, letting the air cool his heated skin.

He wasn't sure how much of this he could take in one evening. The last thing he needed was to get involved with his partner. If he wasn't careful, he'd find himself courting disaster.

Shifting into gear, he saw her reach up and lock her door. "It's not necessary to do that you know."

She didn't answer. Just stared at him with those big brown eyes.

"This is Willow Junction, Charlene. There's nothing to be afraid of. Heck, I don't even lock my house."

"You don't? Aren't you afraid you'll be robbed?"

"Never gave it a thought."

"That's because you're a man. It's not the same for a woman."

If it was possible, she looked even more pale as she fingered the hem of her shirt.

"Would you feel better if I locked my door?" he asked.

With a look of relief, she nodded, answering, "Yes, thank you."

He locked the door. "Are all New Yorkers this fearful or is it just you?"

"It's not unusual to have two or more locks on your apartment door, to carry mace, a whistle—"

"But there's more to your fear, isn't there? Anything to do with your broken arm and bruises? Your hospital stay?"

When she didn't answer him right away, he glanced at her. She stared straight ahead, chewing on her lip.

"Yes," she finally said. "I don't like remembering that night, but I can't forget it either. I was mugged."

Logan frowned. *Mugged?* How did he not know that? Logan waited the few minutes it took to reach the truck stop, pulling into a parking space and shutting off the ignition before responding. He turned toward her. "You were attacked?"

"Yes."

He put a hand on her cast, moved his hand down to her exposed fingers, then squeezed lightly, wishing he could remove the frightened look from her face. He knew about her life only from what little Charlie had told him. Now he wanted to know more. Once again, he found himself wishing harm to the person who had done this to her, who had made her this nervous. No one deserved to be hurt like this. He felt her shudder. "Come on," he said, opening his door. "Let's get you inside where it's warm."

Settled in a booth, and their orders taken, Logan pressed her softly, "Can you tell me about it?"

She took a deep breath, determined not to relive the fear. She was safe now. "I'd just arrived home from London. While I've always been cautious, I've never felt in danger while traveling. The taxi had just dropped me off. My arms were full, and I was juggling my suitcases. I had my dry cleaning, a few groceries, and I wasn't paying attention, looking around is my habit. Suddenly, I heard someone running. Next thing I knew, I was in the hospital with a broken arm and a concussion."

"You were robbed?"

"Only my watch. The only jewelry I wear. A present from the Maestro on my first tour. My shoulder bag wasn't touched, though I had a couple other bags over it. Neither was my luggage. Nothing else was taken."

"The guy ought to be made into dog meat," Logan growled. "That's why you weren't at the funeral."

She nodded. "I was in London when Gramps died and

when the Maestro finally got a hold of me. I got on the first plane home, planning to come to the funeral. I was in the hospital instead. I wish I could have been here for him."

"He wasn't alone, Charlene."

She looked at him. He was telling her he'd been with Gramps when he died. "I'm glad. Thank you."

With the arrival of their meal, she leaned back against the backrest of her seat. She looked up from her plate just in time to see Logan give the waitress a wide smile.

Her breath caught in her throat. Lines radiated from the outer edges of his eyes like sunbursts as he and the server conversed, and he smiled at something she said. Hearing his deep rumbling laughter, Charlene felt an unexpected quickening in her lower abdomen.

She wished it was her he was smiling so broadly at, not this woman who was old enough to be his mother. Picking up her fork, she concentrated on stabbing a French fry.

The server was gone and in two bites, Logan's hamburger was nearly half gone.

"How does your boyfriend feel about your being here?"

"It's not a problem."

"He doesn't mind?"

"No, I don't have one."

"No one?"

"No."

"That's not what the papers said."

"You mean the tabloids, don't you? Don't believe everything

you read."

"Why is that?"

"He was my manager. I thought he was my friend. For a while, I thought there was more. He took—stole every dime I had."

"You're better off without him. He wasn't your boyfriend?"

"Robert and I were together all the time. Everyone took it for granted that we were a couple. I guess I did too. Though, now, I realize I thought of him more as a brother than anything else. Too late, I found he had cancelled my health insurance months earlier, nearly a year earlier—why I don't know. More money in his pocket, I assume, or he just didn't renew for some reason. Now I have a mountain of bills to pay for."

"I'm sorry."

"What hurt more than anything was that I trusted him and he betrayed me."

"And why you're finding it hard to trust anyone."

"Something like that."

He didn't like that she was lumping him into the same category as everyone else. "What about your arm? Are the doctors right?"

"The tabloids again. I wish people would stop reading that junk. No," she said emphatically. "The doctors weren't right. My career isn't over. I *will* be playing the piano again. Having to stay here for six months is probably for the best. My neighbor, Mike, is closing my condo for me. He takes care of the birds whenever I'm gone. Fortunately, the condo is paid for. I'm hoping the sale of the furniture and Gramps' house will be enough to pay the bills without having to sell the condo."

"I want to buy the house."

Charlene's hand stilled. "Why? I'm sorry. It's none of my business why. What I mean is, you don't have to do that."

"I want to. I rent the house I'm in now, and my landlord won't sell. I like being close to the orchard. I was born and raised here. I want real roots. To own my house. Believe me, it's not just to help you out."

With Norton having told them about the value of Charlie's estate, they agreed upon a price.

"Of course, the deal won't be final until the six months have passed, but I'll have Norton draw up the agreement," she said.

Logan offered his hand across the table. Charlene put her right hand in his. It was a business seal of their deal, but suddenly it was much more. Nothing had changed, yet when she looked at him, she could tell he sensed it, too. Her heart skipped a beat. She pulled her hand away first, before her senses spun any further out of control.

How's the hamburg?" he asked.

Charlene bit into it. She expected it to taste like sawdust, much like everything else had lately, but she was surprised. She chewed and swallowed.

"Good. Tell me about yourself. You know so much about me. You said you weren't married." She saw his eyes darken, a frown appearing. "Girlfriend?"

"No. No girlfriend."

"Parents? Grandparents?"

"Neither. My parents had me late in life. My grandfather was still alive at the time, but they're all gone now. Like you, I was an only child. I don't think my parents really knew what to do with me. They left me to my own devices most of the time. Living in such a small community, what could happen, right?"

"I get the impression you managed to find trouble."

"It had a way of finding me. I guess I didn't realize how much trouble I was headed into until your grandfather took me under his wing. He saved my butt really."

"How's that?"

"My parents died—were killed in a car accident. Grandad took me in, but he didn't know what to do with me either. He tried his best. In the end, I was taking care of him. He was a retired veteran and because of his back, he couldn't work. Hell, he couldn't do much of anything. I learned real fast how to cook and clean house. A few years later, I got some chickens and started a garden. It was that or we went to bed hungry. That's when Charlie gave me a job. About that time, the guys I'd been hanging around with started stealing and burglarizing. Six months later, every one of them was in jail. Had I still been involved with them, I'd have been in jail with them."

"Where are they all now?"

Logan shrugged. "Don't know. Don't care. It's part of my life I'd rather forget." Logan wondered how she'd gotten him to open up like that. He never talked about his past. Ever.

"Gramps must have seen something special in you. He must have known that you were a worker."

"I had no choice. Instead of playing football and dating, I was making repairs to our house and putting food on the table."

"You must be every woman's dream of a handyman."

"Not to all of them," he said gruffly.

She saw his jaw harden. The way he tightly gripped his coffee mug, Charlene wondered what woman had hurt him so badly that he'd react this way. She wanted to reach out a finger and trace the line of his jaw, wishing she could soften the look on his face. She had a feeling he'd rebuff her if she tried.

"Ready to go?" he asked.

She nodded and slid out of the booth. Standing next to him as he paid the bill, she was aware of the looks the servers gave her. The way the women scrutinized her, she figured they'd never seen Logan with a woman on his arm before. Considering what Logan had told her, she wondered if it *was* unusual for him to be seen with a woman.

Once they were on the road again, she asked, "Does the orchard occupy all your time?"

"Most of it except during the winter months."

"Do you have another job?"

"I do odd jobs off season. Construction, remodeling, building cabinets, that kind of thing. Once people found out I could make repairs, they had me rebuilding, or adding a room onto their homes. It's a good living, so I can't complain. But, I can't understand why folks want to renovate. If I had my way, I'd build brand new, with modern fixtures and huge windows."

"You really meant it when you said if it were your choice,

you'd get rid of Gramps' furniture and start with something different."

"Yeah, I meant it. It's old, dark, and heavy."

"But refinished, it'll be beautiful again."

"No thanks. Generally, as far as I'm concerned, collecting anything whether it's furniture or baseball cards is a waste of time. My whole house could go up in flames and it wouldn't bother me. Life's too short to accumulate possessions and spend the rest of your life protecting and preserving everything. However, that said, I'll refurbish the house the way your Grandfather would have liked, keeping Vera's—your grandmother's memory alive. But, it will be modern in some features and easy to maintain, at the same time."

"Good. For a minute there, I was beginning to think I'd made a mistake selling you the house. You're awfully young to have such a harsh attitude about older styles to have come to that conclusion." She realized that once he owned the house, she couldn't dictate any changes. As much as she would keep the aesthetics the same, she suspected he'd make more changes than she would.

"Thirty-one isn't that young. If you haven't learned what you want by then, life can be a hard road. It's hard enough as it is without trying to keep everything as it was."

"And, what is it you want in life?"

"To own my own business free and clear."

"The orchard."

Logan didn't say anything. He didn't have to. She knew

exactly what he wanted, or rather what he didn't want. Her as a partner.

Now that they were back in her driveway, she felt exhausted. The last two days—the week—were catching up to her.

Logan opened her door and extended his hand to her to help her out. She looked up at him and was pleased to see the companionable man whom she had come to appreciate earlier had returned. The hard look was gone, replaced with a warm gaze. The moment she touched him, though, his gaze changed and she didn't know why.

She shivered. Not from being cold but knowing she'd have to watch her step with this man. She had a sense that he could be her salvation or the path toward destruction.

After he helped her out of the car, he released his hold on her. As he walked her to her door, she realized she didn't want the evening to end. She wanted to learn more about this man. She wanted to know what was beneath the hard exterior he wore like a protective armor. It'd been a long time since she'd had the opportunity to enjoy being with someone like this. Especially one of the opposite sex and one as good looking as Logan.

"What are you going to do about your car?" He motioned to the rented car.

Charlene sighed. "I guess I hadn't thought about it. I need to return it now that I'll be staying here."

"You can drive my car while you're here. I doubt you'd be able to drive Charlie's old pickup. It's a stick shift. It can be tricky with or without a cast. Not to mention its fickle motor. It's stored in the shed back there." He pointed to one of the out buildings.

"You sure it won't be an inconvenience?"

"Not at all. This pickup belongs to the orchard. As long you don't mind me driving it all the time."

"No. That's fine with me."

"Shall we return the car tomorrow?"

She nodded.

"How about I come at ten and follow you to a rental place that's closer than the Detroit airport. I'll make the phone calls to learn where."

"Thank you. That would be a big help, but I'm not taking you away from anything, am I?"

He hesitated. "Not really. Nothing that can't be put off until later. I need to run some errands anyway. Plus, we can talk about the orchard after we return the car."

"Would you like to go eat again tomorrow night? Maybe get some pizza in the big city?"

"Big city?"

"Marshall. On our way home."

She laughed at his connotation of big city. If she remembered right, Marshall's population was barely seven thousand.

Needing a few simple supplies, she said, "Yes."

"We'll make a day of it then."

"A day of it," she echoed.

Logan opened the screen door, then opened the house door for her. She stepped over the threshold and turned to face him.

"Thanks again for everything, Logan."

His blue eyes, glimmering in the soft porch light, were compelling and magnetic. Like beacons of light on the sea on a dark and stormy night. She leaned toward him, to give him a kiss on the cheek. To thank him for everything he'd done for her today. Nothing more.

His breath whispered softly across her mouth.

He turned his face and brushed his lips against her. Soft and tentative, tasting like mint. She trembled. He pulled away.

She opened her eyes and gazed at eyes now shadowed, any emotion hidden in the depths.

"Good night," he said softly.

She echoed his words. "Good night."

She eased the screen door shut, but stood behind it, watching him return to the truck, which he had pulled up past house to unload more easily at the back door. He opened the door, stopped, looked her way, got in, and shut the door.

The engine roared to life, the headlights blinding. Gravel spit as the tires spun slightly before catching hold. Seconds later, only dust remained.

She started to shut the inner storm door, then hesitated. She wasn't ready to turn in. Thinking about the kiss, she brushed away any thought that there was any feeling behind it. He had moved. It had been nothing more than a mistake. An accident. Nothing more.

Turning off the porch light, she stepped back onto the porch. An owl hooted in the distance, and another responded to the call. She sat on the glider, one leg tucked beneath her, pushing off ever so slightly with her other leg. Frogs croaked somewhere in the distance.

Maple leaves rustled against each other in the trees. In another month, the woods would be ablaze in brilliant color. Honestly, she thought, chastising herself, one would think she'd never seen fall before. New York had its share of fall color. Granted, Central Park was pretty in the fall, but it wasn't the same. She had to leave the city to admire nature's vast canvas of paints. It wasn't like she'd ever been deprived of the brilliance of the fall season.

Her thoughts returned to Logan. She didn't want to be attracted to him, but she was. A sexual attraction, nothing more. He was an attractive man with a compelling aura. Hadn't she seen how the girls had turned their heads at the restaurant, and how he didn't even notice?

She hadn't come here for a relationship nor did she want one.

In the end, there would be nothing but heartbreak. She had her career; he had his whether they remained partners or not. It would be best if they just remained friends. Nothing more.

When mosquitoes started biting, she slapped at them, got up, went inside, locking first the screen door, then shutting the heavy wooden door and locking it. She paused, wondering if she really needed to lock the screen door. No, she had every justification wanting security right now. She leaned against the old solid oak door, her gaze taking in the hall and the rooms that led from it.

Six months. Right now, it loomed like an eternity. Not much more could possibly go wrong. It already had.

* * * * *

The next morning Logan sat in the cab of the pickup in Charlene's driveway contemplating the day in front of him. Last night his suggestion of offering her the use of his vehicle, plus helping her deliver hers back to the airport had been a good one. Now, in the light of day he was second guessing himself, especially after he'd gone and kissed her. *How stupid!*

She was his neighbor now, his partner. Yet, he couldn't just leave her to fend for herself. She was a stranger to these parts. It was the neighborly thing to do.

Why were his thoughts about Charlene becoming more than just neighborly? He wanted to run. He didn't want any trouble. Especially not the kind he'd had before. So, why had he kissed her? She had been going for his cheek. He was the one who made it more personal. *Idiot!*

The truck clock read ten. Time to move.

He got out of the truck and rounded the corner of the house. He saw a large vase of fresh cut flowers sitting on the porch. It stopped him in his tracks. Just then the door opened.

He noticed Charlene looking at him first and then the flowers.

"Hello, Logan. Did you do this?"

He admired her trim figure as she bent over to pick it up but struggled because of its size.

He went up the steps and grabbed it for her. "No, it wasn't me."

"Must be the welcome committee here in town then. I was in the shower. I must not have heard them knocking."

"Charlene. We don't have a welcome committee."

She stiffened and paled. "There's not... then... maybe there's a card. Can you bring it in for me?"

Logan followed her through the door, down the hall, and into the parlor. "Just put them there on the coffee table." She went to the bird cages and pulled off the sheet that had covered them during the night. They ruffled their feathers appropriately but were otherwise silent.

Charlene went to the flowers, turning the vase one way, then another, poking through the varied colored stems.

Finally, she saw a small cream-colored envelop buried deep in the bouquet. There was nothing on the outside, no business name, nothing. Inside was a card. It read: *Wishing you a speedy recovery. A fan.*

Charlene flipped the card over hoping there'd be a store name somewhere. Anywhere. There wasn't.

He didn't like the way the color that had been in her cheeks when she'd first met him at the door was now gone. Her face was completely devoid of color. "Charlene? What's wrong?"

Charlene bit her lip. "Nothing." Only Mike and the Maestro knew exactly where she was. No one else knew. No one.

She'd find out later that someone had deposited the bouquet on a wrong doorstep, that's all.

She pasted a smile on her face. "Wherever they came from, aren't they pretty?" She looked at Logan. Her smile became genuine. He looked scrumptious in jeans and a pink pullover shirt. It was an awful color for most men, but on him...

If she thought he looked good, his scent, his aftershave was making her dizzy. Between the fresh scent of morning that had followed in his wake, the flowers, all mixed with that wonderful scent of cherry chocolate again, she knew she wasn't capable of a rational reaction to anything. His still-damp hair curled around the edge of his upraised collar. Her fingers itched to tame the curls.

She needed distance. Picking up her bag, she announced, "I'm ready."

* * * * *

Hours later, the car returned, a stop for a few toiletries and supplies she knew Gramps wouldn't have at the house, and a couple other errands for Logan, they sat across from each other in a booth at a local pizzeria, waiting for their large pepperoni pizza.

Charlene raised her glass, took a slow sip of water, watching Logan over the rim of her glass. Despite herself, she couldn't keep her gaze away from him. If only he had a wart on the end of his nose, was balding, or had a paunch.

That annoying strand of hair was on his forehead again. Her palm grew moist just thinking of moving it. Instead, she unrolled her silverware, and wiped her good hand on her napkin. "I've been curious about something, Logan. When Norton read us the Will, you weren't surprised. How come?"

Logan paused, his forefinger clearing a path through the

condensation on his glass. "After Charlie died, I had to go through his desk looking for a contract he'd made with one of our customers. I came across a copy of his Will. When I saw my name on the first page, I read it."

"And?"

"And what? I'm not sorry I read it."

"No, you're only human. If I'd been in your shoes, I probably would have read it, too. I meant, what was your reaction?"

Logan took a deep breath, scrunched his mouth, then relaxed. He let the breath out. "Honestly? At first, I was mad as hell. He knew how much I wanted to buy the orchard. We'd been talking about it for a month. But, every time I suggested we put something on paper, he'd divert the conversation to something else. Charlie always shot straight from the hip; he never played games like this. One of the reasons I liked him so well. Guess I didn't know him as well as I thought I did."

"What do you mean?"

"I thought the orchard was his primary concern," Logan said.

"What makes you think it wasn't? Because he left me half?"

"Why didn't he leave it all to you? Family was important to him."

"Because you'd been with him since you were a teenager, I would think. Obviously, he thought of you as family, too."

Just then, their waitress placed a piping hot pizza between them and a plate in front of each of them.

"Be careful," she said. "It's hot."

"Thanks, Doll," Logan said.

The waitress grinned at him.

All day, Charlene had noticed once again how Logan's natural friendliness had all the clerks, especially the women, reacting the same way. He oozed charm naturally, and yet he didn't appear close to anyone.

"Is there anything else I can get for you?" the woman asked.

"If there is, we'll let you know, Toots." Logan said.

She laughed and left.

"Doll? Toots? Isn't that a bit—?"

"Dolly's her name. We grew up together. Toots was a nickname I gave her back in grade school."

"As in a secret meaning?"

"Maybe."

"Meaning you're not telling."

"Exactly."

Realizing she wasn't going to get any other answer, Charlene bit into the food. Instantly, she regretted it. Her mouth on fire, tears formed in her eyes. Grabbing her drink, she gulped, mixing it with the food, hoping to cool it down. Fast.

Logan grinned at her. "Too hot?"

Finally, able to swallow, she gasped and choked. "Yes."

His eyes twinkled. "She told you it was hot"

They ate in silence for a few minutes.

Finally, Logan cleared his throat. "About the orchard. What are your intentions for the year?"

"I don't know. I haven't decided. How do you feel about

having me as your partner?"

"I'm not happy about it. You're a concert pianist. What do you know about apple orchards?

"I can learn."

"It took me years to learn the entire operation, the industry, about our competition."

"You could teach me."

"To what end? After your six-month housesitting stint is over, you'll be going back to New York. You'll be involved with your own career. It'd be easier if you just do your thing, and let me have free rein to run the orchard as I see fit."

"And what would that be?"

"To start buying some new equipment, something Charlie wouldn't let me do."

"Why not?"

"Because it cost money. Charlie preferred the old ways. He didn't like making changes."

"But if the orchard operates with a profit... I don't understand."

"The way Charlie ran the orchard, it made a profit and it stayed in the black. Barely. Now, just one disaster can put us in the red. We don't have a lot of surplus capital, nothing with which to purchase new equipment. It's all old and falling apart. We're not only at the mercy of the weather but on the ability of the machinery to operate properly. When we break down, the entire harvest process comes to a halt. We're doing far too much by hand. It increases the cost of labor. A little money spent now will save lots of money later."

"Anything else?"

"Yes. I want to modernize the buildings. When it rains, everything leaks. The salesroom needs to be expanded. Actually, it needs to be torn out. I think the studs are rotted. It'd just be easier to start over and build a modern salesroom. It can be done cheaply enough with corrugated steel paneling. Fortunately, the freezers are in good condition. "Charlie was content enough to let me run the day-to-day operations, but if we're to make a profit and compete in the market, we've got to make improvements."

"As I've said before, I'm not Charlie."

"You are more than you know. Just as stubborn. He couldn't see good sense when it came to the orchard when it was plopped down right in front of him." He leaned toward her and lowered his voice. "And I daresay neither can you."

Charlene leaned across the table until they were practically nose to nose. His eyes were almost her undoing. Though his irises were blue as lake water at high noon on a muggy summer's day, the pupils were as black as a pond on a moonless night. If she wasn't careful, she could get lost in those eyes. "No judgements or decisions until I look at the operation and the books," she said.

His pupils dilated and his nostrils flared. Slowly, they both retreated, straightening. Finally, one side of his mouth turned up. "So, when will you do your looking?"

"Day after tomorrow soon enough?"

He picked up his glass and lifted it toward her. She picked up hers and clinked it against his. They both drank.

Over dinner, she learned more about the business.

Finished with their meal, they left. As a result of their combined errands, the cab was filled with groceries and other items that couldn't endure the wind if stored in the bed of the pickup. Charlene slid under the steering wheel and sat in the middle of the seat, conscious of the pressure of Logan's thigh against her own as he shifted gears, his muscles hard and sinewy. She moved her left arm, resting the cast in her lap.

In minutes, the cab was toasty warm, and she found herself relaxing, listening to rumble of Logan's voice. He pointed out landmarks and the different farms of people she'd soon meet during her stay.

Abruptly, Logan said, "I don't want our personal lives affecting our business decisions, Charlene."

"I don't either."

Logan turned the pickup into her driveway, shut off the ignition, then twisted in his seat so he faced her. She was acutely aware of his arm that lay along the top of the seat and behind her head.

"I don't want you to hesitate to call if you need anything."

"I won't."

"Promise?"

"Promise."

She couldn't look away. And, neither could he. He moved closer, just a fraction of an inch. Her lips parted. The air crackled with anticipation. The vein in his throat throbbed as his heartbeat increased. The windows were fogging and it was warm inside the cab.

Chapter 4

Logan turned and opened his door. Cool evening air rushed in. Surprised at his turn and the sudden rush of air, she straightened. The temperature had dropped. He got out of the truck and waited for her to move over and exit, giving her a hand.

After Logan brought in her supplies, he told her he'd have his car parked in the driveway first thing in the morning. Then, he said good night and left.

Now that he was gone, the house was eerily empty. Too quiet. Not knowing if there was a radio in the house, she started putting the few groceries away in silence. Then, she decided just to put away the refrigerated items. Everything else could wait until tomorrow.

Charlene stopped herself short. She was racing around, her heart pounding, like she was frightened. Of what? She paused, listening. Nothing but silence. She could barely hear the birds in the other room. Her condo was an open concept. Here, the walls created a silence she wasn't used to and it bothered her. She was used to hearing constant noise. Traffic, sirens, door shutting, horns honking.

In the dining room, the large dark rectangle of glass next to the table yawned ominously, her gaze riveted to the inky depth beyond. She wasn't on the third floor of her Brownstown anymore where she didn't have to shut her curtains because of the trees. Though she did shut them during the winter more because of the cold than anything else, here she was on the first floor and anyone could be standing out there, looking in. She'd have to remember to shut the curtains at night. She wasn't used to seeing total black outside her window either.

She snapped off the light and stood waiting for her eyes to adjust. Feeling a bit foolish for being so skittish, she went to the window and peered out. The sky was filled with stars.

Reaching out, she placed her right hand on the cool glass. She pressed her forehead against it too, welcoming the cold sensation against her skin. Threads of cool air wafted between the window frame and the house. With a frown, she placed her hand against the stream of air. It was a bad draft. She'd have to remember to talk to Logan about it.

Lace curtains were decorative but far from functional. Apparently, Gramps and Gram never saw the need to block anyone from seeing in. The house was surrounded by nature with no visible neighbors. Mentally, she made a note to add shades to her list and to remember to measure the windows for them.

She turned away from the window, her gaze taking in the

kitchen and the rooms beyond. She sighed. There was so much that needed to be done.

With only the light from the hall, Charlene rummaged through a couple kitchen drawers until she found a piece of paper and a pencil. "Shades," she said, starting a list. "Contact antique dealer. See Norton about sale-of-house agreement." She put the pencil down. It was a start.

She went to the front door, double checking the lock. Then, she went into the front parlor to cover the birds for the night. They ruffled their feathers at her presence. When she picked up their cover, they spoke in unison. "Good night."

"Good night," she echoed. She grinned. They never failed to make her smile at the end of the day when they did that. With her good hand, she covered their cages.

She didn't like how adept she was becoming with her handicap. While she liked not feeling horribly hindered, she was still frustrated at not being able to play.

She turned, her gaze stopping on the upright piano in the corner. It teased at her.

Seconds later, her hand caressed the smooth mahogany wood. Remarkably, its surface hadn't aged as dark as the other furniture in the room. She lifted the fallboard.

Her fingers touched the keys. Automatically, she played a few one-handed scales. Without thinking, she sat down, running her right hand up and down the keyboard. Though she doubted the piano had been played in years, it didn't sound too badly out of tune.

Minutes later, she ended her one-handed version of "Somewhere, Out There," a song she'd fallen in love with when she'd first heard it. As the resonate sounds faded away, she sighed. She loved her music so much. It couldn't be taken away from her. It couldn't. Her arm would heal and she'd be better than ever. Wishful thinking, for sure. In six weeks, she'd know.

Six weeks and six months. Just a mere speck in one's lifetime, but the time created a crevasse so wide, she wondered if she could cross it successfully. If she let it, this tumultuous time could overwhelm her.

Determined not to wallow in self-pity, Charlene closed the fallboard. She'd be back at the piano regularly during the next six months, even if she had to one hand it for a while.

Realistically though, Charlene knew the piano would have to come later, after her arm had healed. Now, she had the bigger chore of getting the house in order and learning about the business. There was a lot to be done and too much at stake.

Logan was right. Their personal feelings, no matter what happened in the future, would have to be kept separate from business.

The way she'd been thrown in Logan's lap and he in hers, it was only natural that they'd find each other interesting at first. They were partners, feeling their way around each other. Nothing more.

Actually, she felt more about Logan than she wanted to admit, more than what was good for either of them. Despite what they had both agreed to earlier, their personal lives could very well get in the way of their business relationship.

And now that she thought about it, there was something Logan wasn't telling her, something she had sensed tonight and earlier today. The way he was warm to everyone but held back so much of himself. Almost as if he wore invisible but protective armor.

Her judgement of people had always been pretty good. Up until Robert, that is.

Maybe after the six months were up, she would decide to keep it all and remain partners. Except, she'd sold the house already. Truth be known, to keep the orchard would do nothing but complicate her life.

At the entryway, Charlene looked back into the room. After fixing up a bedroom, this would be her first project. The room needed natural light, the dark heavy drapes taken down and something lighter. While she could appreciate that the heavy drapes kept out the cold, they were too heavy for her taste. Looking at the windows, she wondered if they needed to be replaced. Possibly, but she wouldn't be doing it.

The piano was already the focal point of the room but in a sloppy way with all the Victorian-like furniture, heavy area rug and drapes. Most of the plants on the piano were dead and needed to be next to the windows. She could see it now in her mind's eye, the walls a light color, sun streaming in, the plants tall and healthy.

With a flick of her finger, Charlene turned out the light and the one in the hall as she made her way up the stairs.

Finally, in bed, she found herself staring at the ceiling. As tired as she was, she should have dropped right off to sleep. Instead, her thoughts drifted over the day, each of them ending with her new partner.

Logan.

She had been wrong. The different emotions she had felt as a result of his kiss last night hadn't been a one-time event. She had felt the stirring of emotions again tonight when he didn't kiss her. She had expected him to kiss her and was strangely disappointed when he didn't. Why?

She wasn't a naive teenager, but she didn't have the experience some women her age had either. Surprisingly, she was still a virgin and now glad of it. At first, she hated how she never dated when young and then when she was dating, they never seemed to hang around long enough to get intimate.

The older she got, the more she decided that she wanted to give herself to the man she knew would love her for a lifetime, but she wondered if there was such a thing anymore, what with marriages ending so quickly in divorce these days. Her own experiences in dating were bizarre to say the least. Rarely was she able to find time alone with someone who was interested in her. They had to fit into her life, and unfortunately, no one had. As a result, the few men she had gotten involved with couldn't get past her celebrity status.

At first, it was always laughable to them the way they'd be interrupted when they'd go out to eat or just take a walk. After a while, however, their egos couldn't take playing second fiddle. She had waited with her virginity because the emotions hadn't been right. She had liked them but never really loved them.

After those few experiences, she had poured all her energy into her work deciding to postpone marriage until much later in life, if even then. So far, she'd been happy without a man in her life, and she'd seen enough marriages within her symphony family go sour that she felt confident she was doing the right thing. She had thought Robert would be the one. He'd understood her schedule, her career. Fooled her.

Now?

Her feelings about Logan gave her pause. Or was it because it'd been a while since she'd been with a man she was attracted to?

Tomorrow would be different.

Determined not to lose any more sleep over the man, Charlene punched her pillow, turned on her good side disrupting Cat who had been sleeping between her legs, and closed her eyes. She reached out with her injured arm and petted Cat with her fingers. He started purring. As she drifted off to sleep, she mentally added more chores to her list.

* * * * *

After checking on the freezers, Logan parked in his driveway, sitting there for the longest time, chastising himself. He needed to get a grip on his emotions. No, it wasn't emotions. It was lust. Pure and simple. They hadn't known each other long for there to be emotions. Oh, heck, who was he kidding? That image of her from long ago was burned into his memory. She'd had a natural look unlike anything he'd seen in the girls he knew, and now, the woman who sat across the table from him tonight, whose leg next to his in the truck had burned his through his jeans, fascinated him. Oh, hell, there was nothing pure and simple about any of this. If only Charlie had finished their negotiations before dying. Why had the old man been so obstinate, changing the conversation every time he brought up wanting to buy the orchard. Charlie was no dummy. What had been his plan?

* * * * *

The next morning, after she'd had her first eye-opening cup of coffee, uncovered the birds, and let Cat out, Charlene called her doctor in New York and explained the situation. Once he made a recommendation with a promise to send her records on, she called the recommended doctor in Marshall, explaining her cast was to come off in about six weeks. Just as she suspected would happen, an appointment was made for a week later, anticipating her records would be in his office by then.

Her next call was to Mike, to enlist his help in getting some clothes to her—a care package of underwear, shoes, sweaters, and a coat. Mike and his partner, Jimmy, kept her in style, so she knew he'd pack according to her needs now.

She thought about calling an antique dealer but then decided to put it off until she'd done a more thorough inventory of the house.

An hour later, dressed in casual cotton slacks and a blouse, Charlene grabbed her purse and her shopping list, which had grown considerable overnight for things forgotten, including the purchase of a few clothes she hadn't thought to get yesterday. Her regular wardrobe would be out of place and inappropriate for the work ahead of her. Jeans and T-shirts were in order here. Plus, now that she had taken a better look at the kitchen's cupboards and refrigerator, she knew what she needed beyond the basic milk, bread, and eggs she had bought yesterday.

Rounding the corner of the house, Charlene found a light blue mid-size car waiting for her rather than a sporty car with a powerful engine that she had expected Logan to be driving.

Sliding into the seat, Charlene fastened her seatbelt, her gaze taking in the leather interior and the instrument panel. Immediately, Logan's scent overwhelmed her. And, the smell of chocolate was strong. Flipping the switch for the defroster to defog the window, the scent became stronger. The memory of his kiss came to mind.

It was obvious Logan had cleaned the interior; it was spotless. Except for a brightly colored piece of paper under the seat, she noticed. She pulled. It wouldn't budge. Cardboard, rather than paper, it appeared to be jammed under the seat. She tugged harder. This time it gave.

She held up a kiddie fast food container from McDonald's, the kind that always held a little toy along with the meal. He must have loaned the car to someone with kids, she thought tossing it on the floor of the passenger side for now. Charlene put the car into gear determined to put Logan out of her mind.

None too soon, the post office building appeared, a small brick building surrounded by cars and trucks.

Quickly, she parked the car and got out inhaling a deep breath of fresh air. Not like New York at all. Outside, on the sidewalk, two different pairs of people were chatting with mail in hand. She went through the heavy wooden double doors. Inside, the post office was crowded. The foyer held a stamp dispensing machine, a photocopy machine, and mailboxes lined the walls. People stood in clusters around the garbage can disposing of their unwanted mail.

For such a small community, Charlene was surprised to find she had to wait. Though there were two stations, there was only one clerk at the counter. Everyone else was in the back, busy sorting mail. The clerk was tall like Logan, but there the similarities ended.

Finally, it was her turn.

"Good morning. I need to have my mail forwarded here."

"Good morning, Ms. Walker."

Charlene blinked. She never could get used to people recognizing her everywhere she went.

"I'm Jim Mulberry. I left some flowers on your porch yesterday."

"That was you?"

"Why, yes, didn't I sign it?"

"No, it only said *a fan*."

"I'm so sorry. I am a fan and I meant to sign my name."

"They were beautiful. Thank you."

"They came from my wife's garden. Ex-wife... We're divorced. I got the house. Here's the form you need. Just put it in the mail slot when you're finished. It'll take a couple days before you start getting your mail."

"Thank you. I need some stamps too."

He got a book of stamps out and handed it to her. "Do you have the keys to your grandfather's box? The mail isn't delivered at your place. Everyone picks their mail up here."

She took the key ring the lawyer had given her. "His key is probably here."

"May I?" Jim asked, reaching for the ring.

She nodded and handed him the ring.

Quickly he found the key, isolating it from the others and handed it all back to her.

"Thank you."

"Would you be interested in going out to lunch?"

Taken aback, she answered automatically. "I'm sorry. I'm afraid I can't. I'm so busy right now, you know, trying to get moved in." She smiled. He was a fan and she learned from experience that fans weren't the best people to date. She didn't want to appear rude, but she didn't want to encourage him either. "Thank you for asking, though. How much do I owe you?" Finished paying, she moved to one of the tall tables in the center of the room, turning her back toward him and concentrated on filling out the mail-forwarding form.

Done, she dropped it in the slot as Jim had directed, glad to escape from the sudden claustrophobia she felt. The room was crowded with people. Or, was her sudden claustrophobia because of Jim's familiarity? At least now she knew where the flowers had come from.

By the time she'd driven to Marshall to shop for items on

her list, things she'd forgotten the day before, she'd managed to put aside any thoughts except those of the tasks at hand. Staying busy was the only solution to getting through the next six months.

After she cleaned out the farmhouse, she'd find something else to do. Maybe Logan didn't want her at the orchard, but she was entitled to be there. Besides, she wanted to learn the business inside and out. It was her inheritance, her right. How else could she make any sound judgements about the business until she knew more about it?

Home again, Charlene dumped her packages inside then went out onto the back porch. In another few hours, the sun would be setting, and she wanted to take advantage of the swing while the weather was good.

Winter would be here soon enough. She looked across the orchard trying to imagine it covered with snow, its color white and pristine rather than the dirty piles she was used to seeing on street curbs.

Sunlight sparkled through the filter of the maple trees leaves as she moved the swing slowly back and forth. In a month, the trees would be brilliant with color—red, orange, and yellow. Then snow. It would be strange not being in New York for winter. Not seeing Central Park dusted with snow, watching ice skaters, and seeing the lighting of the tree at Rockefeller Center.

As she surveyed the property, she listened to the relaxing silence. She wondered how she would adapt to the slower lifestyle. No people hurrying, rushing around. No horns honking, people staring past her, neon lights everywhere, the sounds of jackhammers and construction.

All she heard now were sparrows chattering as they flittered around in the nearby bushes, the squawk of an occasional blue jay. Several squirrels, running through the trees, caught her attention. She watched as one squirrel ran down the trunk of a maple tree, ran part way across the yard, then started to dig. It was only then that she saw the sizeable nut he held in his jaws. The hole dug, the squirrel made his deposit, covered it up, then scampered away.

Just then Cat jumped up onto the porch. He seemed to have a habit of hiding in the bushes that lined the porch, sitting patiently, sometimes as long as an hour, waiting for that opportune moment to snag a sparrow. So far, she hadn't seen him succeed, and she was glad.

Jumping up onto the swing, Cat climbed onto her lap, circled around a couple times, then plopped down in a relaxed coiled position, his head on his tail. He looked up at her through squinted eyes.

"Comfy?"

He purred.

"Hello."

Charlene looked up. A blond-haired little boy who didn't look old enough to be in school yet stood on the bottom step. She hadn't heard him approach.

"Hello," she said.

He climbed one step and stopped. "Who are you?"

"Charlene Walker. Who are you?"

He climbed another step and stopped. "Brian."

"Are you lost, Brian?"

He climbed up the last step and stood at the edge of the porch. "Nope."

He was a cutie. He moved toward the swing. "I came to feed Cat. Is he hungry?"

"No. Tired, I think."

Charlene slowed the glider so Brian could crawl up onto it. Once he was on, she pushed the swing into motion with her foot. "Where do you live?"

He pointed a small finger to the bushes that lined the yard behind the house. "Over there."

A young man of many words, she thought grinning. Looking at him, she knew he'd be one heck of a heartbreaker one day. He was adorable. Blond hair kept falling into his face. Blue eyes looked up at her, huge and filled with wonder. She wondered who he belonged to, but before she could ask, Brian was talking again.

"Did you know him?" he asked.

"Who?"

"Charlie."

"Charlie was my grandfather."

"Can I call you Charlie?"

"If you want to, but I think it might be confusing to people. It might be better if you called me Charlene."

Brian reached a hand out and petted Cat. Cat raised his head and tilted his head toward the hand that scratched him, moving his head around so he'd be scratched everywhere.

"What's that?" he asked pointing to her broken arm.

"A cast. I broke my arm and this thing keeps me from moving my arm. Here," she said, taking his hand and placing it on the cast. "It's hard. You can knock on it and it won't even hurt me."

Brian did and looked up at her in astonishment. "Wow."

She smiled. He looked up at her again and stared at her mouth.

"You both have funny teeth."

"Who does."

"You and Charlie."

She opened her mouth a little and put a finger on a tooth turned slightly sideways. "You mean the twisted one?"

"You twisted it?" Brian opened his mouth wide and put fingers from both hands on a tooth of his own and tried to twist it.

She laughed and reached out to pull his hands away from his mouth. "No, that's not how. I didn't wear my retainer like I should have and—"

"What's a retainer?"

"A thing that keeps your teeth straight just after you've had braces removed from—"

"I know about braces. Hannah just got hers off. She said they hurt. Do they?"

"Only in the beginning. You get used to them." She looked around. She couldn't see any houses nearby. She wondered where he lived and if he was telling the truth about being allowed to come feed Cat.

"Who is Hannah? Your sister?"

"No. I don't have any brothers or sisters. Wish I did."

"How old are you?"

"Five. I get to go to school next year."

"Do your parents know where you are?"

"No. Dad wasn't home when I left."

"Who's Hannah?" she asked again.

"She watches me."

"What about your mom?"

"I don't have a mom. She left us when I was a baby."

"She died?"

"No, she left. That's what dad said."

"Brian!"

Charlene's head snapped up. Shock ran through her. Logan was in the yard near the bushes, where Brian had pointed, and was moving toward the porch.

Chapter 5

Was Brian *his* son?

Logan's face looked like an ugly thunderstorm ready to unleash its tumultuous power. Her foot stilled, and the swing stopped moving.

Brian shouted, "Hi, Dad!" He jumped off the glider and his side swung crazily back and forth, while her side stayed stationary with her foot planted solidly on the porch floor. Brian ran toward his father and leaped off the porch. Logan caught him, a grin on Brian's face. The child was clueless his father was upset. Was he upset because Brian hadn't told anyone he was coming to her house?

He spoke gently to Brian as he set the boy on the ground. "Hannah's looking for you."

"Okay." With motions resembling skipping but looking more like hopping, Brian started across the lawn. Not seeing his father behind him, he stopped.

"Go ahead," Logan said. I'm right behind you."

Logan turned back to her and stared. Now she knew what a sparrow felt like just before Cat pounced for it.

Finally, when she could no longer see Brian having disappeared into the bushes, he said, "Leave my son alone." He turned and started walking away.

Charlene jumped to her feet, setting Cat on the ground. "Hold it right there!"

Logan stopped, turned, and looked at her with a steady gaze.

"You've got a lot of nerve telling me not to hurt your son. What do you think I am, a monster, the new neighborhood child molester?"

Logan looked down, took a deep breath while running his hand through his hair. He looked back up at her. "You're right. I'm sorry. I'm protective of him. I don't want him hurt."

"It's not my intention to hurt him. He's a sweet kid."

"He shouldn't be bothering you."

"He's not a bother. We were just getting to know each other, though I have to admit it's a shock finding out he's your son. How come you didn't tell me?"

"It didn't come up in the conversation."

"And why is that? I asked about your family."

"You asked about my parents and if I had any brothers or sisters.

"Not telling someone you have a child is quite an omission, wouldn't you say?"

"I've got to go." Logan turned and left.

Flabbergasted, Charlene watched him disappear into the bushes. First, he knew about the Will but pretended he was hearing about it for the first time at the reading, then last night as they talked about themselves, never once mentioning his son. Of course, that explained the box she'd found in the car this morning.

It was also obvious that Logan still bore the pain of his wife leaving him with a young son.

What else was he hiding?

A cold chill brushed past Charlene. She shivered, wrapping her arms around her. Cat sat at the door, waiting to be let in. She opened the door. Cat scampered in and she followed.

The birds fed, Charlene went into the kitchen, found Cat's food, filled his bowl, and fixed her own dinner—a bowl of vegetable soup and a grilled cheese. With limited use of her hands, her meals had become simplistic. She stood at the stove, her gaze going to the window and the back yard and to the bushes that separated their two yards.

Brian had said his mother had left. The other day Charlene had wondered who had hurt Logan to make him so bitter. Now she knew—Brian's mother. At least, Brian didn't show any scars, but what about Logan? He had enough scars for the both of them.

She wondered what had caused Brian's mother to leave, deserting her husband and son as she had. It was obvious by Logan's hard attitude that he felt betrayed, that it had been his wife's fault. Was it?

Between that experience and his childhood, she could see

why he was reserved about people. More than ever, she was curious about this man who had become her partner.

* * * * *

The next morning, Charlene headed for the orchard. It was time to take a look at the other property she had inherited. At the orchard, she parked the car in front of the old wooden building that she remembered as the salesroom. If she thought nothing had changed at the house, here time had stood still completely.

She could picture Gramps now, coming out the door to greet her. When the door to the salesroom opened, she half expected to see Gramps. Instead, it was Logan.

Her heartbeat quickened, and she inhaled deeply. Big mistake. Her nostrils filled with the chocolate cherry scent that teased at her senses. With shaky fingers she reached for the door handle.

He stood at the door, waiting. Watching. She walked toward him, suddenly conscious of every movement.

His gaze traveled up and down, taking in the casual outfit, his gaze lingering on her hair.

"How do you do that with your arm in a cast?"

Her free hand went to the knot at her nape. She shrugged. "Habit, I guess. It's not difficult."

"Didn't really expect you today."

"Hoping, don't you mean?"

He held the door open for her.

Instantly, she smelled the apples, crisp and fresh. The place hadn't changed at all. The same monster cash register sat on the wooden counter. Crates of apples, all tipped at a slight angle to expose the contents to the customer, lined the walls. There were so many varieties to choose from. Cooking apples and eating apples, all in various shades of reds, plus the yellow Golden Delicious and the ever-popular green Granny Smith apples.

There were boxes of candied and caramel apples as well. Indian corn tied in bundles hung on the posts. There was squash, mostly summer and longneck, and decorative gourds spilling out of baskets. And, there was cider and packaged donuts. It looked like fall in here despite the unseasonable warmth outside.

A woman entered the room through a doorway that Charlene knew led to the storage room, the freezers, and the back entrance. Her dark hair was cropped short and curly, and she wore jeans, boots, a white shirt, and jean vest. All she needed was a Stetson to complete the outfit. Close on her heels was a man—well tanned from the sun—about Logan's age. They both stared at her.

Logan introduced her. "Charlene, this is Josie Miller and Alan Slayton. Josie manages the salesroom; Alan is my foreman. I couldn't run the place without either of them. Josie, Alan, this is Charlene Walker."

"Charlie's granddaughter?" Alan asked.

"And Logan's new partner," Charlene added. Alan and Josie's looked at each other, then in unison their gaze swung back to Logan.

"Ah, Logan," Alan said. "You need to come back to the freezer and take a look. The temperature appears to be rising."

To Charlene, Logan said, "Josie can show you around. I'll

91

catch up with you later."

Once they were gone, Charlene said, "I don't think he's too happy that we've been made partners."

Josie laughed. "I *know* he's not. But, don't let that bother you. He'll get used to it."

"But, will I?"

"Get used to Logan?"

"No, get used to owning half an orchard." She doubted she could ever get used to Logan in any way. Not even as a partner in business. "The salesroom hasn't changed much, has it?"

"You've been here before?"

"A long time ago."

Josie rearranged some of the gourds. "You're right. Nothing has changed. Charlie preferred it that way."

"And Logan?" Charlene wished she could take the words back. It wasn't fair to use Josie like this, obtaining information she should be getting from Logan.

"Logan wants to tear this room down and put up something more modern, more eye appealing."

"And, what do you think?"

"Honestly? I think the wiring needs to be updated and the room could be expanded, but I like the look of it. It's country."

"It would be a shame to lose the charm of the room."

Several women entered the saleroom and Charlene stayed in the background while Josie waited on them, packaging their purchases of apples, cider, and doughnuts.

"Do you sell any crafts?" one lady asked.

"No, I'm sorry we don't," Josie said.

"That's a shame," the woman said. "You've got the perfect location. We just came from a craft show. We're always looking for something new." Several of the other women nodded their heads in agreement.

Another woman spoke. "My granddaughter is expecting a baby and I'm looking for a baby quilt. She and her husband just moved into a beautiful log cabin, but she doesn't have the time to go to the craft shows like I do."

Moments later, their transactions complete, the women turned to leave.

"Thanks for stopping by," Josie said, as they left.

When the door closed behind them, Charlene asked, "What did they mean by crafts?"

Josie shut the cash register drawer, "Oh, quilts, dolls, wooden toys and things like baskets, bread boxes, anything that's handmade. And, we're talking about quality items, not junk. Haven't you ever been to a craft show?"

"Not really. Antiques are my thing."

"There are also several booths of antiques at these shows. One of the best shows I can think of is during the annual Home Tour that Marshall holds every year. Lots of booths plus the stores downtown."

Logan and Alan returned to the showroom. Logan clapped Alan on the back. "Thank for keeping out an eagle eye. Go ahead and order the part. Once it's installed, everything should be okay."

"I'll get right on it." Then Alan left.

Logan turned his attention to Charlene. "Been on the tour already?"

"Actually, no."

Josie said, "We got busy. We were just about to do it."

Car doors slamming outside had them all turning toward the windows. "Looks like more customers, Josie. I'll take Charlene around."

He took her to the back rooms first.

"These are the freezers, right?" Charlene said, indicating the large doors. "I remember Gramps telling me this was where the apples went to bed."

"To sleep actually. The apples we sold all summer and most of which we're selling now are from last year's crop. Another couple of weeks and we start harvesting this year's crop. "The process is called CA. Oxygen is removed from the apple and carbon dioxide added. If stored properly, the apples that have been *put to sleep* can be stored for as long as two years. To wake them up the process is reversed."

"I had no idea. Guess I took my fruits and vegetables at the grocery store for granted."

"Most everyone does."

Moments later, they were out back behind the building, surrounded by huge bins and piles and piles of crates. From where she stood, three heavily-used lanes, apparent from the lack of grass, extended out like spokes on a wheel. Everywhere she looked was fruit trees, all heavily laden with fruit. The trees weren't tall — only about ten to fifteen feet. But, they were nearly as wide as they were tall.

They walked down one of the lanes between two rows of trees.

"How come there are so many bare spots?" she asked.

"You mean like a tree should have been there?"

"Yes."

"This is the oldest orchard. See how thick the branches are. Most of the trees here are over fifty years old. As the old trees died, new ones get planted. If you look closer, you'll see there are younger trees here and there.

"A tree is at its peak production when it's about eight to ten years old. After a tree passes its fortieth year, it slows down. Just like us."

"You don't appear like the type to slow down."

"Neither do you."

Charlene stumbled. Logan caught her, one hand on her waist, the other on her elbow. She looked up at him, more acutely aware than ever how large a man he was. Today his eyes matched the blue in the sky exactly. It was hard to look away.

"Are you all right?"

She nodded. She didn't like feeling this way about Logan. Tongue-tied, heart racing, palms moist every time he touched her. It left her feeling vulnerable. Vulnerability was a weakness and more so now than ever, she didn't like feeling weak.

Pretending to straighten out her shirt, she ran a hand down her front, wiping her palm on her slacks. "Yes, I'm fine."

Several workers in the orchard had stopped work and were

watching.

"Why are they looking at me so funny?" she asked.

When Logan looked their way, they all turned back to their work.

"Probably because you didn't come to Charlie's funeral. In a community this size, we take care of our own, like family."

"And here I was, Charlie's actual family and I didn't show up."

"Something like that. I told them you'd been in an accident. They were probably checking out your cast."

"Are these regular employees?"

"No, seasonal workers. Getting ready for the harvest. After the harvest and once winter arrives, Josie, Alan, and I pretty much handle everything. Even then, Josie and Alan only work part-time. I wish I could hire them full-time."

"Why can't you?"

"Not enough money."

"Is it really that bad?"

"Come take a look at the books. See for yourself."

An hour later, Charlene saw everything Logan had said was true. She closed the ledger book. "So what happens?"

"You tell me. Got a magic genie?"

"Believe me, if I did, I wouldn't be here now. Isn't there anything we can do?"

"Yeah, but I don't think you want to hear it."

"Tell me."

"We borrow more money and invest in new equipment."

"No. No borrowing."

"You've got to spend money to make it."

"But, we don't have it. I don't have it. The orchard needs to be self-sufficient. Other than my condo in New York, I don't own anything else and I'm up to my eyeballs in debt. I was relying on the orchard to help me get out of debt."

"The business can't endure that kind of load."

"You said *borrow more money.* What do you mean by more?"

"We already have one mortgage."

"You're kidding? After all these years?"

"We had two bad years in a row, a tornado took half the trees in the back orchard. We were lucky we didn't lose any of the buildings. Just the roof on the main building. We won't be able to afford another disaster like that."

"What about insurance?"

"Charlie depended on the odds. He only had a minimum of insurance."

"What about now? How well are we covered?"

"Excellent against mother nature, but not against competitors and regular breakdowns."

Charlene sighed. "We're getting nowhere."

"Nothing's going to get resolved in one day, though, I think you need to reconsider our borrowing money."

"For new equipment?"

"Used, but newer than we have, and it'd be used as the collateral."

"Do we have a choice?"

"Not really."

If she wasn't his partner, he'd be free to do what needed done. She'd be taking a risk to trust him so readily but having seen for herself how smoothly everyone worked together, how clean the equipment and buildings were kept, she had to trust that, so far, he'd been a good manager. Wouldn't that mean he'd be an even better owner?

"All right," she finally said.

The next couple hours were spent going over ads for different machinery, setting up a plan. Logan admitted they couldn't get everything done right away, but if they could get one or two replacement pieces cheap, they might be able to improve their ability to harvest.

"Let's hope we haven't waited too late," he said, as he walked her to the car. "Why don't I come over tonight to take a look at your chimney and furnace, and I'll let you know how I did then?"

Charlene agreed.

Minutes later Charlene was back home, unlocking the front door. Instantly, she heard Stan and Ollie's silly chatter. Here, in larger surroundings, they didn't sound nearly as noisy as they had in her small condo. She stuck her head into the parlor to check on them. Seeing they had plenty of water, she went on into the kitchen.

There, the silence was unnerving. She needed some noise to keep her company. Finding a portable radio in one of the bedrooms, she brought it into the kitchen and turned it on to a station featuring the *Oldies but Goodies from Yesteryear.*

With her good hand on her hip, she looked around the kitchen. Might as well start here. Like the other rooms, there was too much stuff in here. The counters were full of crocks, appliances, and dishes. Apparently, her grandfather had found it easier to store the dishes he used frequently on the counter than on shelves behind closed doors. Though, once she opened all the cupboards, she reasoned he'd done so because there was no room. Charlene preferred cleared spaces, keeping her possessions to a minimum. With all her time spent with her music, she'd found it easier to keep house if she kept things simple.

Looking up, Charlene decided to start with the upper cupboards. She retrieved the step-ladder she'd seen in the pantry and started emptying them out.

An hour later, she'd managed to unload two cupboards. It was slower going than she had imagined. First, because there were lots of dishes packed into the cupboards, and second, because of her arm.

Determined to at least get the other cupboards unloaded, Charlene concentrated on what she was doing. It hadn't taken long before she'd established a rhythm. Grab what she could with one hand, bend over, deposit it, then start the process all over. The only difficulty she developed was with the very top shelves that forced her to take a step up to get the dishes, and take a step back down to unload.

A third set of cupboards finished, she started with the next top shelf. She hummed with the music.

With a large platter in her hand, she started to step down to place it on the counter when the music stopped suddenly.

She twisted around. The plate dropped, crashing to the floor, breaking into fragments, and she started falling.

Horrified, she couldn't stop herself.

Suddenly, strong arms were around her. Instinctively, she fought, but his hold was too tight.

"Whoa. It's me. Logan."

Instantly, she stilled.

He lowered her to the ground, her body sliding against his. His belt buckle pulled her top up as she slid, and the metal rubbed against her bare belly. And then, she felt the rasp of his jeans against her linen pants. For just an instant, they were knee to knee, heart to heart.

Her heart beat wildly. Her fingertips rested against his chest, and she felt the rapid beat of his heart. Her casted arm was crushed between them.

She looked up. His eyes smoldered. She couldn't swallow, breathe, or move. This close, she could see every hair of his shadowed jaw and chin and each dark lash that framed blue eyes that reminded her of the center of a hot flame. Fine lines crinkled like starbursts at the corners of his eyes. There was a slight bump she hadn't noticed before on an otherwise straight nose. But, it was his lips that fascinated her.

His breath fanned her face, tingling every nerve, the sensation traveling throughout her body until she thought she would melt from anticipation.

Time stretched unbearably.

Finally, he moved away from her.

His eyes changed. They became the eyes of a stranger. He'd put up a shield of some kind, blocking her out, shuttling his desire away.

"That was a stupid thing to do," he said.

She pushed herself totally away from him, and dusted off her pants, trying to slow her heart rate at the same time. "To fall, I agree."

"No. To be up on that footstool with a broken arm."

Her head snapped up, and her eyes narrowed. "If you came here looking for a fight, why don't you just leave? I've got work to do." Turning her back on him, she put a foot on the stool, ready to climb it again.

A hand on her arm stopped her. "Let me help."

"Why should I?"

"Because I made you fall."

"Why did you turn the radio off?"

"Because you were so engrossed in what you were doing, you didn't hear me call you. First, let me get the broom and sweep up this mess."

Moments later, Logan was up the ladder. Charlene didn't remember giving him permission to assist her, but now that he was here, she was glad for the help. He could remove the dishes faster than she could, so it was stupid to argue with him.

At the speed he was emptying the shelves, she wondered if he was trying to exorcise a few ghosts of his own, just as she'd been doing. Being active had always been her way to forget issues at hand.

With no dishes coming down, Charlene saw him scanning the shelves.

"All done." He started down. She held up a sponge. He stopped. "For me? You shouldn't have."

She smiled, then laughed.

"You should laugh more often," Logan told her. For a few seconds, the desire that she'd experienced earlier was there again, only this time it was softer, not as intense.

Logan smiled. Taking the sponge, he went back up the steps. "I'm to wash the shelves, right?"

"As long as they're clear, might as well. Unless you'd rather wait and do it later."

"No. Now's as good a time as any."

"I'm not planning on using them. I'm just going to keep what few necessary dishes and utensils I need to get by and dispose of all the rest."

While Logan washed the now empty shelves, Charlene tried to organize the dishes into some kind of order. All she managed to do in the few minutes it took him to wash the shelves was to stack the plates. Logan dropped the sponge in the sink. "Done."

Charlene looked around the room at the rest of the dishes. Cut glass, Depression glass, old utensils, cast iron bakeware, pitchers, and trays covered every conceivable surface like ivy under a shade tree. It was everywhere.

Logan whistled. "Looks like you've got your work cut out for you."

"I can't thank you enough for your help, Logan. It would have taken me forever to unload all this off those shelves, though I didn't mean to keep you like this."

"You didn't keep me from anything. I came to check the furnace and chimney originally, but it's too dark now. If nothing else, I saved you some work. Will you be able to find a market for all this?"

"I hope so. Logan, about the house. I only expected to be here for a few days. Now those few days have turned into six months. I can't live here for six months with the house in this condition."

"No, I couldn't either," he said looking at the mess. "Fixing a meal with everything like this would be a real challenge."

"That's not what I meant. I'm talking about the house as a whole. It's too dark and drab. I doubt Gramps painted or papered anything since Grandma died."

"What did you have in mind?"

"I want to lighten up the rooms with paint. At least redo the rooms I'll be spending the most time in, most especially this room. This green is nauseating. It must have been Grandma's favorite color. It's everywhere. If the furniture isn't green, the rugs or the walls are."

"Guess I never really noticed." Logan folded up the ladder and stored it in the pantry.

"I'm asking you because the house will be yours in six

months."

"Tell you what. I'll bring some paint chips by tomorrow and I'll buy the paint. But no painting until the cast comes off."

"Logan, I'm not helpless. I'll admit I can't move furniture, even boxes, but how much effort does it take to paint trim and a wall or two?"

"All right, all right. You win. Just give me your word you won't push it. That if you need any help, you'll ask for it."

"Agreed."

If only they could agree that easily about the orchard. Charlene had a feeling when it came to the business, things would get worse before they ever started getting better. She had agreed today that the orchard needed additional machinery, but she wasn't sure it was the totally right thing to do. Only time would tell.

"You know, you don't have to do this," Logan said. "Let me do it."

"Logan, I want to. I have to do it. I'll go stir crazy with six months and nothing to do."

"Then, you've decided to leave the business of running the orchard to me."

"Not for a minute."

"But you just said—"

"Logan. Once before, I gave all my financial responsibilities to someone else, and I knew him quite well. I don't know you. At least, not well enough to give you that kind of freedom. Don't ask me to. Having made that mistake once before, I won't be making it again."

Logan took his time responding. "What is it you expect to do then?"

"Honestly? I don't know. I think we made a start today. By the way, how did you do with the equipment ads?"

"We're right back to square one. Everything and anything I was after, I was a day late and a dollar short."

"Sold?"

He nodded.

"Now what?" she asked.

"I don't know."

"I'd like to work with Josie in the salesroom, if that's all right with you. If we worked at it, we could complement each other as partners."

"Like hot fudge on ice cream?"

"Why do you think Charlie made us partners?" she asked.

"Your guess is as good as mine."

"You have no idea, not even a guess?"

"Not a one. I know that he talked about you often. He was proud of you, and he missed you."

He'd been proud of her. "I should have made an effort to see him more."

"Why do you keep beating yourself for something you had no control over? You said before you couldn't visit like you wanted. Charlie understood."

"What about you? You offer me advice that you yourself don't take. Why do you keep beating yourself up about your past?"

Chapter 6

She saw him stiffen. "You're skating on dangerous ice."

"Why did your wife leave? Was it because of Brian?"

His eyes darkened, and now, his mouth resembled a slash. The instant she saw his mouth tighten, she knew she'd gone too far, but she wanted to know. What had driven the woman to the point of abandoning her husband and newborn son?

Granted, Logan rattled her. His sexuality overpowered her anytime they were close. He was protective of his son, he treated his... *their* employees fairly, and he'd been more than helpful to her in the kitchen. And yet...

He swallowed hard, his Adam's apple sliding up, and down. Then, he tilted his head back, closed his eyes, and sighed. Suddenly his body relaxed, he lowered his head and opened his eyes, his gaze strong and steady. All she saw now was poignant pain.

"I had no warning. She just left."

"No clue whatsoever?"

"Oh, she complained now and then of being lonely. Apparently, it was more serious than I knew." He went to the sink, flattened his hands on the countertop, resting his weight on them.

Finally, he turned, leaned against the counter, and crossed his arms. His eyes lightened and the corners of his mouth lifted slightly. "She was a knockout. A woman every man desired—blonde, sultry, and the preacher's daughter."

"Wild you mean?"

Logan raised his eyebrows and grinned knowingly. "No more than any preacher's child. But yes, there was a wildness to her. And yes, it made her attractive. "Beth and her family moved here from Texas, and lived in Willow Junction for three years before we fell in love during her senior year. There were some who told me I was making a mistake. I was four years older. Her parents approved of me but wanted us to wait, but Beth wouldn't hear of it. We eloped the day after her graduation."

"Did you regret eloping?"

"At the time, no. Now, I don't know. It certainly wasn't my idea to have her just up and leave like that."

"Where did she go?"

"She always talked about Florida. Miami, in particular. She hated winter. The final divorce papers she had signed and returned had a Miami postmark. Other than that, I've never heard. Nor do I care."

"She's never come back to see Brian?"

"No."

Charlene was stunned. She couldn't imagine a mother simply abandoning her child like that. "How old was Brian when she left?" she asked softly.

"Just a month or so."

Charlene gasped. "Oh, Logan. How awful. You must have been angry."

"I didn't have time to be angry. I had Brian to take care of. I was fortunate enough to find sitters during the day, but at night, he was totally my responsibility. For the first six months, he was colicky."

What a responsibility he'd had thrust upon him, she thought. "You've done well, Logan. Brian's a delightful little boy."

"I don't want him hurt, Charlene."

Now everything made sense. She moved closer to him, putting a hand on his arm. He was over-protective with Brian because of his own hurt. "Logan, I would never hurt Brian."

"How can you know that? Beth was his mother and she left him."

"I'm not Beth."

"It's hard being a parent, knowing the right thing to do. To this day, I don't know why she left. It could have been me. It could have been the weather for all I know. While she was pregnant, she changed. I didn't know her anymore. I couldn't please her no matter what I did."

"You've got to stop blaming yourself."

He straightened and pushed away from the counter. "I've got to go. Brian will be expecting me to tuck him into bed. Plus, I told Hannah I wouldn't be long. She's going to kill me as it is. I stayed too long. Goodnight."

Logan slipped out the back door. At the door, she scoured the dark yard, trying to see movement of any kind. He was already gone.

Who was Hannah? Another neighbor? A girlfriend?

Whenever Logan was around, her good sense flew out the window. She'd just have to gather what business acumen she had left and use it like a shield. If not, she wasn't sure how many more encounters like this one she could endure.

Picking up the sponge, she rinsed it out and started attacking the lower shelves. She was too restless to go to bed yet.

Going through the dishes that were on the counters and table and those that still remained in the lower shelves and cabinets, Charlene chose a pattern for the dishes she'd use while she was here. The remaining full sets, in mint condition, would be a find for some lucky shopper.

Almost done with the chore of assembling basic dishes for her stay, Charlene stored her chosen set of china, a Currier & Ives in blue, in the cabinet.

Tired of being in the kitchen, Charlene decided to stop. Tomorrow would be soon enough to go through the rest of the paraphernalia and box up what she wouldn't keep.

A glance at her watch revealed it was only nine o'clock. Too early for bed, and she was too restless to sit and read. There was an ancient television in the living room, but she was too restless for it, as well.

With a pad of paper and pencil in hand, she decided to take a quick tour of the house, making notes on what needed to be done. She was good at organization. If the kitchen represented what she would discover in the rest of the house, she'd be plenty busy during the next six months.

Just as she had suspected, every closet, dresser, and drawer was crammed full. There were clothes, linens, photographs, papers—personal and business—magazines, books, and more dishes. She even found a room full of toys, sports equipment, and other belongings that must have belonged to her father while growing up here. He had been an only child, too. She looked forward to going through the room to discover who he was as a kid. After he had moved to the other side of the country, he had called once telling her, he'd be at the airport for a short layover in New York, as he was returning from Europe. Her mother went with her. She had barely recognized him. He died shortly after that. Her mother had been concerned that she was hiding her feelings, but she hadn't been. There was nothing to feel. It wasn't like they'd had a relationship, but that didn't mean she wasn't curious to learn more now.

Cat, who had followed her from room to room sat in the doorway, gave her a penetrating look.

He licked a paw, set it back down, then yawned.

She yawned too. "Quit doing that."

Walking past him, she approached the last door in the hallway. Cat looked at her, then turned his back on her and headed for her bedroom.

"Deserter," she called after him. Her hand on the knob, she turned it, and opened the door. It screeched, and she jumped. It'd been a long time since this door had been opened. A flight of stairs stood in front of her. Looking up, there was nothing but inky blackness. The attic.

She checked for a light switch and found one. Flipping it on, she went up. When her head reached floor level she looked around. It was too dark. The light had been just for the stairwell. She looked for another switch. Instead, she saw a string dangling from the ceiling. Once she was completely in the attic, she reached for it and pulled. She stood in the middle of a circle of light and noticed the corners remained shadowed.

Her eyes widened in surprise and then genuine delight. The room was filled with furniture. More antiques. Forgetting how tired she was, she moved as best she could among the pieces of furniture, most of it piled higher than herself. A Victorian horsehair sofa was hidden beneath rush bottom, ladderback chairs. An old wicker rocker sat on top of a Chippendale dresser. Soon, she lost count. There was everything—beds, dressers, tables, chairs, end tables, a commode, pie safes, a dry sink, and an endless sea of boxes.

Logan would probably call everything up here junk too, but for her, it was like finding a pot of gold. Her goal of paying off her debts suddenly didn't seem so overwhelming.

Judging from the thickness of the dust that lay on everything, the room had remained undisturbed for a long, long time. More than likely, it had been forgotten. Bed slats stacked against one of the many dressers caught her eye. Squatting down next to the boards, she saw they were solid oak. She looked for the bed they belonged to.

A minute later she found what she was looking for. A dismantled early American colonial four-poster bed. Instantly, she knew this would be the first piece she'd refinish, to keep and use for herself. The posters appeared hand-carved. She wondered which room the bed had once belonged.

Smiling, she rubbed her hand across the headboard.

"Ouch!" She jerked her hand back and looked at her palm. Unable to see anything, she rose and moved until she stood under the bare bulb. She had snagged a splinter. A big one. And it appeared to be deeply imbedded in the pad of her right hand, just beneath her middle finger.

Awkwardly, she tried to probe at it with fingernail of her casted hand. The cast stopped at the tips of her fingers, making her motions awkward. Pain forced her to stop. All she was doing was pushing the splinter deeper into her palm. Looking at it one more time, she tried to remember if she'd seen a sewing kit or any kind of safety pins that she could use to dig the splinter out.

Fifteen minutes later, Charlene sat on the corner of her bed frustrated that her attempt to remove the splinter was unsuccessful. Placing the needle back into the sewing box she'd found, she went to the bathroom looking for disinfectant.

Her doctor's appointment was tomorrow. The removal of the splinter would have to wait until then.

* * * * *

Early the next morning, Charlene set out for Marshall.

After signing in and filling out the rudimentary first-time visit forms and returning them to the receptionist, Charlene returned to her seat in the doctor's waiting room. She grabbed a magazine but sat noticing the unusual decor. Baskets were arranged around a table against the wall. Above the table hung paintings done in a variety of media—oil, pastels, and ink. Wooden wall ornaments in various forms adorned the walls, and rested against the table. A goose, duck, teddy bear, and an Amish couple with no faces.

Throughout the room, Charlene noticed smaller items—a basket of dried flowers, a straw hat on a stand decorated with miniature silk flowers, a corn husk doll that carried a basket of apples, and a candleholder that looked like a tin can that had been reshaped and now had intricate cut-outs. And everything bore a price tag.

A nurse opened a door and called her name. Charlene followed her into the hall.

"I was admiring the waiting room," she said. They turned into the third examining room. "Are all those items handmade?"

The nurse indicated for Charlene to sit on the edge of the examining table. "Yes, all locally done." She took Charlene's uninjured arm, tucked Charlene's hand under her arm and wrapped Charlene's upper arm with a blood pressure cuff, secured the Velcro fastener, then squeezed the bulb. Charlene remained silent while the nurse read her blood pressure.

The nurse removed the stethoscope from her ears. "In fact,

you just missed Marshall's Historic Home Tour."

"Someone else mentioned the tour. What is it?"

"Most of the downtown area and many of Marshall's historic homes—over 100 buildings all told—are registered with Michigan's National Historic Society. The first weekend after Labor Day, about a half dozen homes are open for the public. There are art fairs, craft shows, museums, antique markets, you name it. The community explodes with about 12,000 visitors that weekend, doubling our population."

"Isn't it unusual for a doctor to display crafts like this? I mean in his office?"

"Yes, but not for Dr. Hunter. He's a member of the Historical Society. You probably didn't notice the literature advertising next year's Home Tour."

Two hours later, Charlene headed back to Willow Junction. Dr. Hunter had received her files, stating that her arm was healing and that he'd see her in six weeks. They would take another x-ray then, and if everything was still fine, the cast would be removed.

Turning the steering wheel, her palm rubbed against the instrument. Pain jabbed at her.

"Darn it," she mumbled. She'd forgotten about the splinter. Since she was stopping at the orchard, maybe Josie could remove it for her. All she needed was someone with two good hands.

* * * * *

Logan lifted the last of the six bushels of apples into Mrs. Williams' car trunk. Gravel crunched as another car pulled in. From over the top of the open truck door, Logan spotted Charlene.

Even though she wore new jeans, she could have been wearing silk. Charlene didn't belong in Willow Junction. She stuck out like a ballad in the middle of a Rock and Roll festival.

The way she carried herself, her back straight, her shoulders back, gave her an elegance and the appearance that she floated when she walked. He could watch her all day.

Thanking Mrs. Williams for her business, he shut the trunk and waved the elderly woman on her way. For as long as he'd been at the orchard, Mrs. Williams faithfully bought six bushels of apples—the first of the season—every year. And every year at Christmas time, she gave him half a dozen jars of canned applesauce.

He fell into step with Charlene. "What brings you out?"

She held up her cast. "Doctor's visit. In six weeks, I'll be able to start practicing again."

Logan opened the door to the salesroom. Charlene preceded him into the building. She looked around. "Is Josie here?"

"No. She won't be in for another hour."

He saw her fingers rub the palm of her hand. It looked red. Logan reached out and opened her hand. He felt her instinctively pull away, but he tugged and pulled her hand closer. The tips of her fingers were against his stomach. He felt as if she were branding him. Her arm quivered. She stared back at him, her eyes dilating.

He moved his thumb across her palm. She hissed.

"It's a splinter," she said. "I forgot to have the doctor remove it and was going to ask Josie if she could do it."

"I'm able. That is if you want me..."

Her gaze locked with his again.

"...to," he finished. He was a fool to stand here holding her hand, staring into her eyes, but he couldn't stop. She'd been here just a few days and he was smitten with her, turned inside out. Plus, she had turned the community on its ear. Everyone was talking about her. It was only natural with her celebrity status. At the post office this morning, Jim was telling anyone who would listen how he'd met her and how he'd given her flowers. Jealously had never been a problem for Logan in the past, but this morning it had surged through him hot and fast, just like the feelings of desire he experienced now.

He longed to touch her face, to erase the bruises that looked worse today than they did two days ago. The yellowish cast of the bruises lent an even frailer look to her already slight features. The larger bruise on her neck looked sensitive, like it still throbbed with hurt. It'd be another week before they'd completely disappear.

Suddenly, Logan felt he stood on the edge of a yawning precipice. He'd been there once before because of a woman who had left him, and which he had vowed never to be in that position again. The pain was too much, and yet, here he was and it didn't feel near as frightening as he thought it should. Lack of sleep would do that he told himself. Heaven only knew he hadn't gotten any last night all because of the creature that stood in front of him wide-eyed and vulnerable.

"Let's go back into the office. There's a first-aid kit there."

Charlene preferred to wait for Josie, but Logan didn't give

her a chance to answer. Rather than letting go of her hand, he turned and pulled her along with him. Not until they were in the office did he finally let go.

Dangerous ground loomed before Charlene.

When Logan turned his back on her and went to the filing cabinet, pulling out a first aid kit, she wiped her palm on her thigh. The way he'd looked at her had her heart thumping wildly. Even now, it hadn't resumed it's normal slow, steady beat.

The kit in hand, he motioned her to a chair in front of his desk.

Before sitting in the chair next to hers, he bent, his hands on either arm of her chair and moved it around to face him. Surprised at the movement, Charlene leaned back into the chair, her mouth forming a surprised *oh*.

A corner of his mouth lifted at her surprise. If she didn't know any better, she could have sworn he was setting her off balance on purpose.

The kit on the desk, he opened it, and quickly found a pair of tweezers. Facing her, he sat on the edge of his chair, his legs spread wide, her legs inside his, and pulled her closer. Their heads close together, he peered at her hand.

"How'd you manage to get a splinter like this?"

"I was fondling furniture."

Logan laughed. "Looks like it fondled back." He forced himself to focus on her hand instead of picturing her running her hand along the grain of the wood. What he wanted to do was run his hands up her bare arms. Her skin was so smooth.

She gasped when he dragged the sliver out of her skin. The second he had it out, she tried to pull her hand away.

"Does that really hurt or are you afraid of me?"

At first, she wouldn't look at him. When he didn't let go of her hand, she finally looked at him boldly.

"You keep asking me that. No, I'm not."

He moved closer, delighted seeing her eyes widen even further. He was close enough to kiss her. Instead, he stopped, then whispered. "Liar."

Immediately he pulled back and reached for some antiseptic. "Let me put something on that so it won't get infected."

He opened the tube of cream. He had to pull her hand so it rested on his leg. "Stop fidgeting."

"I'm not."

She was fidgeting no matter how much she denied it. Even though her hand lay still, he could see her pulse jumping erratically. He longed to run his thumb along her pulse and sooth her nerves. Only trouble was, if he followed his instincts her nerves would become even more unsettled — just like his were now.

"Brian's been bugging me," he said applying the cream. "He wants to come visit you."

"He's more than welcome. In fact, I'd like the company."

"I don't want him over-extending his welcome. He can be a bother."

"Like his daddy?"

"Do I bother you, Charlene?"

"I'm a big girl, Logan."

119

"Don't I know it." He capped the cream and reached for a Band-Aid. "But you're avoiding the question." He spread the Band-Aid over the wound, letting his thumbs extend past the tabs of the Band-Aid and onto her skin. This time he kept his thumb on her pulse. "I'll ask you again. Do I bother you?"

It was the longest minute in his life. He was gratified knowing her pulse was beating faster.

Finally, she spoke, her voice just a whisper. "You know you do."

He couldn't stop himself. He leaned forward. With only his thumbs on her hand, his thighs resting against her legs, he kissed her. His left hand slid up her arm, over her shoulder and rested under the bun of her wrapped hair as he pulled her head toward him so he could taste her more fully. She was like sweet honey in its purest form.

He pulled back reluctantly, letting his hand slide back down her arm as he retreated.

It had been a mistake marrying Beth. He knew that now. What he thought had been love with Beth was nothing compared to what he was feeling now. He and Beth had been in lust. He couldn't deny it any longer. Having a child had taught him what it was to love unconditionally and he wanted to share that with a woman.

The only trouble was, Charlene wouldn't be that woman no matter what he felt. She had her own agenda.

Looking at Charlene now, he wondered if she'd ever had a serious relationship, one in which she was truly and deeply in love.

With his finger curved, he rubbed her cheek and down her neck where bruises still lingered, barely touching her.

Chapter 7

Charlene wanted to melt into a puddle at Logan's feet. She'd never had a man take care of her so consciously, so carefully, then on top of it all, kiss her so softly, so thoroughly. Her heart overflowed with affection, a warmth stealing over her body unlike anything she'd ever felt before.

Then, he stood and was putting away the first aid kit as if nothing had happened.

"Are you liking Willow Junction?" he asked.

"So far. Everyone seems friendly enough."

She rose, tugging her purse over her cast and onto her shoulder. When they re-entered the salesroom, Josie was closing the cash register. Customers were leaving the parking lot. Charlene didn't remember hearing the bell.

"Logan. I forgot. When I was at the doctor's office earlier, I had an idea. What if we sell crafts here along with the produce?

Homemade crafts that come from local ladies?"

Josie replied enthusiastically, clapping her hands together. "That's an excellent idea. Quilts, corn husk dolls—"

"I don't know," Logan interrupted. "That'd mean more work for you, Josie."

Charlene countered, "But, I told you I wanted to work mornings, Logan. It'd be one way for me to learn about the business. I'd be helping Josie. Think of the community," she continued, hoping to persuade Logan. "Where else can these women sell their goods? And, I was here the other morning when some customers were asking about crafts."

Josie jumped in. "I get people, mostly women, asking whether we have any crafts all the time. Let's try it, Logan."

"What have we got to lose?" Charlene asked.

Logan ran a hand through his hair, then cupped the back of his neck. Finally, he jammed his hands into his pockets. He glanced at the two women. "All right. Let's try it. For a month or two and see how it goes. No promises."

Just then half a dozen cars pulled up and the phone rang. Logan went to answer the phone. Josie was able to help most everyone, while Charlene hung back waiting to help if needed.

After the salesroom cleared, Charlene left.

Home at last, Charlene parked the car, retrieved a sack of groceries and would return for the rest. Walking around the house, she saw Brian on the glider.

When he saw her, he jumped off and ran to her. "Dad called and said it was okay to visit you. I came right over," he said enthusiastically. "What are we going to do?"

Charlene laughed at his impetuousness. "First, we're going to take care of these groceries and everything else out in the car. Then, I've got to feed Stanley and Ollie and clean their cages, then how about we make some chocolate chip cookies?"

"Oh, boy! I know how to make real good cookies. Can I help with the birds too?"

"Sure, you can."

The groceries and birds taken care of and the first batch of cookies out of the oven, Charlene and Brian sat at the kitchen table eating warm, fragrant, still soft cookies. Charlene watched as Brian dipped his into his glass of milk before taking a bite.

"You don't dip your cookies?" he asked. "Dad dips his. Says they're more wholesome that way."

Charlene smiled, imagining the two males, their heads together, dipping cookies and talking. "Who makes the cookies in your house?"

"Me and Hannah. She takes care of me during the day. She's real fat right now. I like her a lot. She smells like strawberries all the time. You do too. How come girls smell like that?"

Charlene imagined Hannah was a middle-aged woman, probably someone's grandmother, taking on the responsibility of looking after Brian because her family was gone. "Because we're girls. Do you like strawberries?"

"I love strawberry shortened cake."

Charlene chuckled at his mispronunciation. "Short cake."

"That's what I said. What are we going to do next?"

"By the time these cookies are done, it'll be time for you to go home. I wouldn't want Hannah worrying about you."

"She told me not to stay too long. What will you do after I leave?"

"I'm not sure. What do you suggest?"

Brian looked around the kitchen. "Probably ought to clean up this mess. Dad would have a fit if I made a mess like this."

Charlene laughed. She could easily imagine Logan saying exactly that. She glanced at the clock.

"I've got a call to make." She looked over his shoulder as he dipped the spoon into the bowl and transferred the ingredients to the cookie pan. "You're doing a good job. Finish the tray while I make my call."

Still keeping an eye on Brian, Charlene dialed the number of the antique dealer from the ad she'd seen earlier. He was still in.

Minutes later, she hung up. He'd promised to come out in a couple days and look at the furniture.

"What's refinish?" Brian asked.

Charlene explained the process to Brian as they finished baking the cookies. By the time he had his coat on and was ready to leave, Charlene had promised him that he could help her in the days to come.

At the window, Charlene watched Brian cross the yard, a box of cookies under his arm. She waved when he turned around and waved one last time. Then, he disappeared through a hole in the shrubbery.

She looked around the kitchen. Brian was right. It was a

mess. She needed some boxes to move some of this stuff off the counters.

Charlene changed her clothes. Several trips later, between the attic and the kitchen, she had managed to retrieve only half a dozen empty boxes. Now she sat on the top step of the attic steps looking at all the stuff up there. There had to be a better way. She needed at least another dozen boxes. They were up here, but this endless carrying only two at a time because of her broken arm was wasting time. She grew even more weary just looking at all the stacked-up furniture and filled boxes, knowing she'd want those downstairs at some time, too.

Getting up, she went and grabbed two more determined to get the job done. At the head of the stairs, one fell and bounced down the stairs. Several minutes later all the boxes lay in a heap at the bottom of the stairs. It didn't look pretty, but she had moved them with very little effort.

Before leaving the attic to repeat the process with the second flight of stairs to get the boxes to the first level, Charlene went back to where the boxes had been. Now, she could get at the bed she'd seen earlier the other day.

Just then, she heard a creak on the stairs. She froze, then a head appeared. It was Logan.

"Darn it, Logan. Don't startle me like that."

"I didn't do it on purpose. Must be you didn't hear me calling out ever since I entered the house. I thought I was making more than enough noise. Brian said something about furniture and I thought you might foolishly attempt moving it on your own."

"Nothing foolish about it. All I'm moving are empty boxes. Now that you're here, I could use your help."

"What can I do?"

She showed him the dismantled bed she wanted taken downstairs into the back bedroom where she'd refinish it.

Charlene scurried ahead of him, opening doors. It wasn't hard for him to move the bed, just awkward. The headboard and footboard were the hardest to move because of the bed posts.

"How are you going to refinish these?" He stacked everything against the wall.

"With a couple saw horses and an old door or something flat I could use as a table top."

"There might be some saw horses in Charlie's shed. Your shed, I mean."

"Your shed," she corrected. "But, I know what you mean. I still think of this as Gramps' house too. I guess it'll take both of us a while. Oops, I better go back up and turn off the attic light."

"I'll go with you to make sure we got the entire bed."

In the attic, Logan moved a few pieces of furniture, but it looked like they'd gotten all pieces.

"Wait a minute," Charlene exclaimed. "Is that a trunk?"

Logan bent down and looked past the table he'd just moved. "Looks like it." He pulled it out, under the light.

Charlene stepped to the front of it, her fingertips together under her chin.

"Aren't you going to open it?" he asked.

"Yes. But, I want to savor the moment, to imagine what

might be inside it."

Logan laughed. "That's a woman for you. Hotter than honey in July about wanting something, then relishing the wait because she doesn't want the surprise spoiled."

She couldn't open it herself. The rust on the latch and hinges told her it'd been quite a long time since anyone had last opened the chest.

Charlene stood behind Logan while he hunkered down and eyed the hardware. "The hinges are so rusty, it's going to take tools to get into this. How much do you care about saving the hardware?"

"A lot even if they're rusty, because they can still be cleaned."

"Got a screwdriver?"

She made a pretense of patting herself down. "Not on me."

Laughing, he headed toward the stairs. "Charlie kept some tools in a drawer in the kitchen."

"Must be a drawer I haven't cleaned out yet," she mumbled.

While Logan was gone, Charlene studied the trunk. It was a treasure to be sure and would command a high price if she decided to part with it. She'd have until the end of the week to decide. That's when the dealer she'd called was coming.

Logan returned. She stood off to the side, out of the light, and watched him attack the stubborn lock with care. Finally, it gave way.

When Logan threw back the lid, her mouth dropped open. On top, wrapped carefully in blue tissue lay a lace gown. Gingerly, she pulled it out. The hem dropped to the floor. It was a wedding dress. Ivory silk and lace. She held it up against her.

"What do you think?"

Logan felt his breath catch. Despite their cobwebby surroundings, the cast, the wisps of hair that had escaped its confined bun, even the smudge of dirt across her cheek that mingled with the last lingering tinge of yellowing bruise couldn't detract from the radiant bride she would make. She gazed at him misty-eyed, very much the way he imagined she would on her wedding day. He envied her future husband-to-be, whoever he would be.

Never would he forget the look of rapture and pure delight on her face as she looked at him right now.

He wanted to crush her to him and hear whispered words meant only for his ears.

"It's beautiful," he said. Then he added, "Just like you."

Charlene gazed at him, her eyes soft and sultry. "It had to be Grandma's." A tear escaped down her cheek.

Logan raised his hand to her face. With his palm cupping her cheek, his thumb slid under her eye, erasing the tear. "Why the tears?" he asked gently.

"I feel so close to them. Gramps and Grandma. I don't remember her. All I know about her was from the stories Gramps would tell." She bit her lip to keep it from trembling. Her glance moved to the trunk again.

Her eyes widened.

"Look, Logan. A journal and a photo album."

Logan grabbed the two books. "You want me to take these downstairs?"

She nodded.

"Anything else?" he asked.

"Are there any more albums?"

Logan rifled through the trunk with care. "No, the rest looks like clothes and souvenirs. And this box."

"What is it?" she asked, moving her head closer to his so she could see.

He opened the lid of the box. A few notes of music echoed in the attic before the sound died.

"A music box. Bring that down too."

They carried the items downstairs, and Charlene led him to the front bedroom, the room she had confiscated as her own. Carefully, she hung the dress on a hanger, then had Logan hang it on the door.

While Charlene found a cloth to wipe the music box and find a place for it on a dresser, Logan observed the room. Despite the old, dark wall paper, he liked what she'd done to the room. She'd found some white lace curtains for the windows and had a frilly white dust cover on the bed, with a folded, colorful patchwork quilt draped on the footboard. He couldn't remember any of the rooms ever showing this much color, but he assumed she'd found everything in the house. He admired how she'd made only a few changes, yet the difference was remarkable. The room was now brighter and more cheerful, though there was still too much furniture for the size of the room.

Musical pings from the music box filled the room. "Rachmaninoff's 'Rhapsody on a Theme of Paganini.' One of my favorites," she said.

Logan took Charlene's good hand in his and put a hand on her waist, moving slowly in a dance.

He felt her hips sway, and her skin felt warm as he held her uninjured hand. His gaze caressed her hair. He ached to touch her. In the light, the cobweb in her hair shimmered like lace, and gave him the much-needed opportunity he desired. He fingered the cobweb and gently pulled at it.

Her face lifted, she looked at him, her brown eyes questioning.

"You had a cobweb in your hair."

"Is it still there?" she asked softly, her gaze fastened on his lips.

"Not anymore." He bent toward her and kissed her. When his mouth touched hers, he felt the strains of music pulse through him. He was lost in the moment.

There was no doubt in his mind that he had drowned and mercifully been brought back to witness the secret of sweetness, only to experience the rush all over again.

A shrill ring rent the air. Logan tried to stop Charlene from responding to it. He didn't want her to leave him. After the phone had rung several more times though, he let her go.

He watched her move away from him to answer the telephone by the side of her bed. She held the phone out to him.

It was Hannah. When he hung up, Charlene was dusting

the photo album and journal.

"Hannah's ready to go home."

"Thanks for your help with the bed."

He chucked her under the chin and gave her a quick kiss on the lips, wanting more but content to continue this later.

* * * * *

Locking the door behind him, Charlene leaned against it. Despite knowing this relationship wasn't going to have a happy ending, she couldn't help herself. It felt good. He felt good. He smelled good and was a natural at kissing. She sighed and pushed off, heading toward the kitchen to turn out the lights.

She couldn't think about where they were headed. All she knew was that in six months things were going to change and in a big way. All she had to do was live in the moment. Ever since gaining notoriety with a high demand for more concerts, she had always lived months in advance. Right now, it felt good to cherish each day as it came.

* * * * *

At the orchard the next morning, Charlene entered the salesroom, waving to Josie who was busy with a customer. She walked into the office. In her hand was a package Jim had given her at the post office. Even though it had the business name and address, the package was personally addressed to Logan. Laying the package on the desk, she noticed rolled papers—papers that resembled plans.

Curious, Charlene unrolled them and puzzled over it. Finally, it dawned on her that she was looking at the salesroom and the building. A modernized version.

Her mouth spread into a thin line as she studied the plans. The salesroom was as different from its present form as the moon was to earth.

The door to the office open. Startled, Charlene straightened, her hand jerking away from the desk. The paper rolled back up on its own.

Logan stopped mid-stride. Charlene saw him look at the desk, then back at her.

He stepped into the office, shutting the door behind him.

"I hope you don't mind that I looked," she said.

"No... no." He tossed the papers he'd been carrying onto the edge of the desk, circled around her, and dropped into the seat. She moved to the only other chair in the office and sat down, imitating his casual manner. "I'll admit when I first came in the door, I was surprised, but this is your office too. It's the only office we have. I've got nothing to hide. I see you've noticed the plans."

"Yes."

"What do you think about them?"

"Honestly? I don't like them."

"Somehow I'm not surprised.

"How long ago were they drawn up?"

"Before you arrived, when Charlie and I were negotiating. Or, so I thought. Guess I was looking at them hoping you might change your mind, that you'd be receptive to modernizing the building. What's this?" he asked, indicating the package she had laid on the desk.

"From the post office."

"Thanks."

"I haven't changed my mind, Logan. In fact, in thinking about the crafts, I think we need more than ever to keep a country look. It could be a draw. Besides, every time I come here, I see Gramps. If you want to modernize the rest of the operation, I won't stand in your way, but I disagree with your plans for the salesroom. This is the room the customers see, what they're attracted to."

Logan released the corners and the paper rewound itself back into a roll. She watched him pick it up, roll it, secure an end with a rubber band, and toss it aside.

"Why are you so against the country look?" she asked.

"Because it looks old."

"Not if it's done right. We're in the country and people coming here expecting to find country. It can be charming. Look at Marshall. When I was there the other day, I went to the different stores, heard more about the Home Tour, saw what attracts thousands of people. We can duplicate that look right here with what we've already got. Speaking of which, what are we going to do with that bad wall?" she asked.

The other day he had shown her the wall in the salesroom, that needed repair, more than likely replacing. The rest of the salesroom was solid and in good shape.

"Wait until spring to fix it. We've already started our busiest season and colder weather is just around the corner. It's waited this long. One more season isn't going to make a difference. We do need to talk about the motor on the forklift, however. That can't wait. It either has to be replaced or repaired."

"I would say repair it," Charlene said.

"Before you decide, you need to know that the motor is thirty years old and the repair may cost as much as to buy a new one."

"Can you still repair the motor and use it somewhere else in the orchard."

"Not really. It's worn out."

"Where will the money come from?"

"They're going to give us ninety days' credit. I've done business with these people in the past.

"Let's hope the crafts take off."

Charlene left Logan to help Josie. While Charlene waited on customers, Josie called the area women she knew who created the crafts they wanted to display and sell. Soon Josie reported all the women loved the idea and promised to bring their goods by next week.

"I meant to ask you the other day, Charlene. Since you'll be in Willow Junction for a while, would you like to join the local food co-op?"

"What do I have to do?"

"Pay a small initiation fee, then a little work sorting groceries after we eat. I'll show you the ropes. Willow Junction is small so we don't have a grocery store, and this gets you basic supplies without having to run to a larger community all the time." Josie grinned. "Plus, it's a way for us to catch up. With no local newspaper we rely on gossip." She grinned. "Everyone comes straight from work, and we fix sandwiches. No one likes to stay late. I'll pick you up at six."

* * * * *

When Charlene got home, she fixed a bowl of soup and picked up the photo album to browse through it while she ate. At the back of the book, she found black and white, grainy photos of a baby, all of them unmarked.

And then, she saw a photo that captivated her gaze. Charlene recognized the four-poster that she and Logan had carried out of the attic last night. In the bed was a woman, smiling adoringly at a baby wrapped in blankets, snuggled in her arms. A caption read, Johnny's Birth Day."

It was a picture of her grandmother and her father, and the bed where he'd been born. Joy bubbled through her. Now, she knew why the bed had felt special to her.

More than ever, Charlene was anxious to refinish the bed.

She set the photo album aside. Charlie's roll-top desk hugged the wall across from where she sat. It was open and layered with papers. This must have been the desk Logan talked about where he'd found Charlie's Will. Walking over to the desk, Charlene pulled out the chair and sat down.

Drawer after drawer were filled with papers. One by one she started going through them. By the time Josie appeared at her door, she had thrown out hundreds of receipts—phone, heat, purchases Charlie had made, big and little. From all appearances, he had saved everything. Bank statements that went back years, even junk mail. One drawer now held deeds, insurance papers, and notes that had been paid. First thing tomorrow when she went to see Norton to pick up the sales agreement, she'd ask him about the deeds and notes.

Minutes later, they arrived at a white country church.

"It's the only church in the area," Josie said, "but plays a big role in the community. We meet in the basement. It serves as our community center for meetings, reunions, and of course weddings and funerals. The co-op's dues go toward the building's maintenance."

When they walked in, Charlene saw half a dozen people sitting around the table eating tuna sandwiches and potato chips. Logan was one of them. Josie took the chair opposite Logan, leaving the chair next to him for Charlene.

"I didn't know you belonged to the co-op," she said to Logan.

"Didn't I tell you?" Josie said. "Logan's a charter member. In fact, he's the one who initiated the co-op."

"And has the biggest garden you've ever seen," a man across from them said, sticking out his hand. "I'm John Martin." He appeared to be about fifty or fifty-five, distinguished looking with silver hair.

"And he gives most all of it to the co-op," said a young woman at the end of the table, on Logan's other side. She looked no older than twenty. Charlene admired her wide blue eyes and blond ponytail. Cute was a word that came to Charlene's mind.

The blonde spoke again. "I'm Hannah. Nice to finally meet

you."

Other introductions were made, but Charlene found it hard to concentrate as her gaze traveled around the table as each member greeted her. And then, they were back to Hannah. It had to be the same Hannah that stayed with Brian. The Hannah Logan spoke so highly of.

She hadn't expected Hannah to be so young. Or so pretty.

For the most part Charlene listened to the chatter as they ate their sandwiches. She heard how Ed Wilke's dog, Shadow, had finally turned up after being missing for four weeks. And, that Millie Boyette's milk-feed pumpkin—so far, the biggest in the county—was going to be featured on the early morning regional agriculture show on CBS next week.

"Time to get to work," John said.

Logan hurried to Hannah's side. He extended his hand. She took it and he pulled her up.

With the table having hid her bulging stomach, it was easy to see that Hannah was at the end of her pregnancy.

Charlene noted Hannah wore a wedding ring. "When's the baby due?" she asked.

"Not soon enough," Hannah said. "I've still got another month to go."

"And, I can't convince her to take some time off and rest," Logan replied.

"I do rest," Hannah told Logan. "Brian's no trouble at all. I don't want to stay home alone. Mike won't be back until after the baby is born." To Charlene she said, "He's in the military and overseas right now." She turned back to Logan, continuing. "I like the company, and if I didn't know any better, I'd think Brian's been tutored to look after me."

"No comment," Logan said, walking away.

Hannah laughed. "You can't trust those two," she said to Charlene as they both watched Logan move toward the mountain of groceries that needed sorting.

Charlene liked the woman and enjoyed listening to her chatter about her husband, and how anxious they were for the baby's arrival. She could see why Brian was crazy about Hannah.

Josie grabbed Charlene's arm. "Come on, I'm going to take you to your station."

Soon Charlene was measuring a fifty-pound bag of sugar into smaller five-pound bags for those who had ordered sugar this month. By the time she was finished, so was everyone else. She felt handicapped with her broken arm, but no one else seemed bothered by it.

"I've read about such co-ops," Charlene said to Josie later as Josie drove her home. "But, I've never seen one in operation. Logan really cares about the people in this area."

"I think it had to do with his past. We grew up together and for as long as I can remember, he's always gardened. But, as times got hard and the factories laid off more and more of Willow Junction's residents, his garden got larger. And then, he started the co-op. The co-op made the difference during those lean times. We don't need it like we did then, yet we continue. I think mostly because it ties us all together." She turned into Charlene's driveway. "Here we are."

"Thanks for inviting me tonight, Josie."

"I'm glad you became a member. Even if it is just for six months."

Charlene shut the door and waved as Josie turned the car around. As she strolled toward the house, she listened to the croaking frogs and crickets. Soon the cold weather would drive both species into hibernation, and they wouldn't be heard again until spring.

By then, she'd be gone.

Headlights filtered through the trees at the back of the house. Curious, Charlene moved through the backyard, past the trees, until she was at the boundary of her property, on her side of the tall hedge.

She heard voices. One was male, deep and rumbling, the other higher pitched and squealing.

Parting some branches, she peered through the hedge. In the distance, she saw Brian and Logan. Even though it was dark, light from windows illuminated the backyard where they were. So, this was their house. Brian was in a tree swing with Logan pushing him high. With each push Brian laughed loudly. She couldn't see Logan's expression, but if it matched her own, he was smiling too.

Feeling like a voyeur, she moved back, letting the branches fall back into place.

Logan was a good father.

Something sidled up against her ankle. Charlene jerked, wanting to scream but refrained as she didn't want Logan to know she was in the bushes.

Cat meowed and rubbed up against her again. She bent down and picked him up. "Do you know how much you scared me?" she whispered.

Cat purred and rubbed his head up against her chin. She scratched his ears and tucked him under her arm, carrying him back to the house.

Chapter 8

The next day she stopped at Norton's office. The first fifteen minutes, he spent looking at the deeds and other paperwork she'd brought in, telling her none of the paperwork had any value, that Charlie believed in saving *everything*. He reassured Charlene, that the paperwork in Charlie's safety deposit box that he had copies of were indeed relevant and correct.

Now he handed her the sales agreement she had asked for, saying, "Are you sure this is what you want?"

"Yes." She looked at the document and saw it was dated on the day she called him regarding the sale of the house with a six-month closing date. "All we're doing now is waiting until we can close. I don't want the house."

"What about the contents? I noticed there was no mention of the furniture."

"I'm going to sell most of it. I already know that Logan doesn't want most of it."

Norton shook his head. "A shame."

"It is, but time changes everything, doesn't it?"

"Indeed, it does. Something your grandfather hated more than anything."

She nodded and stuck out her hand. "Thank you for everything you've done."

He took her hand, saying, "I wish I could have done more."

* * * * *

The days settled into a routine. Mornings, she'd run errands or work on the house. Late morning, she'd eat lunch, then go relieve Josie so she could eat. After lunch was their busiest time with streams of customers. Late afternoon, she'd return home just in time for Brian's visits. He rarely came empty-handed. So far, he'd brought her weeds in their last bloom complete with roots; acorns with the admonishment if she wanted more, she'd have to find them herself for the rest of his were for the squirrels; a handful of warm M&Ms; a banana; and colored leaves ironed in wax paper. Hannah had helped him with those, he told her as she'd tacked the artwork on her refrigerator with magnets.

Today, he brought pictures he had drawn. With her permission he proudly hung them on her refrigerator next to the leaves.

"Do you really like them?" he asked. They stood admiring his work.

"Yes. Especially the one of the birds flying around the barn."

"Those aren't birds—they're bats. They only come out at night, just before it gets dark. Trillions and zillions of them. Is it time to feed Stan and Ollie?"

"It's time. Go get their dishes." Seconds after Brian ran from the room, she heard him and the birds exchange their usual banter, first cops and robbers, then their exchange of "How are you, I'm fine" routine, and then finally calling the kitty.

Brian re-entered the kitchen and dragged a chair over to the sink where Charlene filled it with water and dish soap. Seeing her struggle with the dishes that first day he visited, Brian had volunteered to help her wash them whenever he was there. With what few dishes she used, and with his help, it didn't take long to get the job done.

Afterward, they started refinishing the bed. Carefully supervising him, she showed him how to sand a piece she'd already stripped, rubbing lightly but in the direction of the grain of wood. And then, she let him apply a small amount of stripper with a paintbrush while she stood over him, watching. Like her, he wore gloves, one of Gramps' old shirts with the sleeves rolled up because of its size, and a pair of safety glasses she had to tie on him because they wanted to slip down his small nose.

"Don't ever come into this room by yourself or the one downstairs where I'm stripping furniture," she reminded him. "The only time you can come into these rooms is when I'm with you."

"Why?" Brian asked.

"Because these are dangerous chemicals, and they can hurt you."

"I won't," Brian promised.

For insurance, Charlene locked the room when they were done. There was no reason to offer temptation to one so young.

"See how the stripper is already bubbling," she said, pointing.

"Is that how it comes off?"

"The stripper is softening the finish," she explained. "In a while, I'll be able to scrap it off."

"Will I be able to help?"

"No, not with that part. It gets really messy. But, you can watch."

The rest of the afternoon passed quickly.

Later, in the kitchen, Charlene watched through the window as Brian ran across the yard, and disappeared into the hedge. She loved the time she spent with him.

As she went about fixing a sandwich for dinner, the evening stretched ahead of her. More than likely, she'd clean out another closet. She wondered if she'd ever finish the job. At this point, six months didn't seem nearly long enough.

While she ate, she noticed the room darkened quickly. Black heavy clouds had moved in. She turned on the light and finished eating and quickly rinsed her dishes, then turned out the light. No use putting it off any longer. Another night, another closet, she thought heading for the front of the house.

A knock came from the front door. Charlene peeked through the curtain. It was Logan. She opened the door.

"This is a surprise," she said. He smelled like the evening air—crisp and chilly. And there was that heavenly scent of chocolate cherry again. He stooped and picked up a box. Her eyes feasted on his broad shoulders as he passed her. With his height advantage and the way he carried it on one shoulder, it was impossible to see in the box.

He placed the box on a table, and she moved around him eagerly.

Quickly, he turned around and put himself between her and the box. She tried to peek around him.

He reached out, grabbing her shoulders, holding her in place. "Why, Charlene Walker. If I didn't know any better, I'd say you were quite curious to find out what I brought you."

She froze, then eased back a step and crossed her arms as best she could with the cast and stood with one hip jutted out, most of her weight on one foot. "Not in the least."

"Not even for these?" From behind his back, he palmed two wrapped cordials.

"How did you know?"

"A little birdie told me."

"Brian."

He offered her one, saw her struggling to unwrap it, took it back, unwrapped it and held it out for her to eat.

She hesitated, then unable to stand the temptation any longer, moved forward to take it from his fingers with her mouth. Her lips brushed against his fingers. Their gazes locked. Slowly, as if in slow motion, she moved back. She bit down. Juice squirted in her mouth, a little bit dribbling onto her bottom lip. She licked at it with her tongue.

Logan's eyes darkened. His gaze feasted on her mouth hungrily. "I was going to have the other, but after that exhibition I think I ought to let you have it. But first..."

He bent and kissed her lightly, tasting the cherry cream.

He straightened, smiling at the luxurious way her eyes looked before her eyes refocused. This wasn't supposed to be happening. It was as if some fairy from one of Brian's books had jumped out of the pages, one who had too much fairy dust and had whacked him over the head, too. He had danced the other night. He never danced. And now, here he was sharing chocolate like he'd never shared it before. It was too much.

Trouble was, he wanted to do it all over again. He left the second cordial on the table. "Look what else I brought you."

"Frames. They're wonderful, Logan."

"Can you use them? I found them in the barn. Brian suggested I bring them to you. Said you could refinish them."

Charlene smiled. "They really don't need refinishing. I'd love to keep a couple of them, but the others could be sold at the orchard."

"Josie told me all the ladies she called were interested in your idea."

"I know. Isn't it wonderful?"

"It would certainly give us another income source."

Logan looked around. The house was beginning to look as if a cyclone had gone through it. There were piles of clothes on the sofa, a huge box of shoes, a stack of boxes next to a table, some half-filled but most of them empty.

"I know," Charlene said. "It looks awful. I start one job, like cleaning a drawer, then get sidetracked cleaning a closet. I've never seen so much stuff. It's been more of a job than I thought it would be."

"Brian said you were working on the bed."

"I've started other pieces down here. In fact, I could use some of your brawn again." She led him across the hall to the dining room or what could have been a second parlor. I'd like to move that dresser in the hall in here."

"Why don't you just sell everything the way it is?"

"The antique dealer was here earlier today and said everything is in mint condition but would bring more refinished but in a country way."

"Country way?"

"Distressed."

"As in been used a lot?"

She nodded. "He said people would rather pay more and have the work already done than to have to do it themselves."

"Where did you learn about furniture?" Logan looked around the room.

"What are you looking for?"

"A blanket."

"Over there. On the floor."

Logan picked it up and spread it on the floor. He opened the drawers satisfied to find them empty. "When I lift the dresser up on that side, slide the blanket under it."

"What's the blanket for?" she asked, doing as he asked.

"Without wheels, I have to drag it. It's too big for me to carry. And with your arm, you can't help me lift it." He grabbed the edge of the blanket, tilted the dresser so only the one edge rested on the floor, then started to pull the whole thing across the floor. It glided noiselessly across the room.

She followed, watching him work the piece of furniture through the doors, observing how he took great care not to scratch the dresser, walls, or doors.

The one hand holding the dresser looked strong and steady, and yet, she remembered how that same hand had gently cupped her face.

In her designated work room, he quickly placed the dresser where she wanted it, taking the drawers out and setting them aside.

"I learned how to refinish furniture from my mother. She'd find old pieces of furniture discarded along the curb or at flea markets. It was a way to earn extra money and pick up nice furniture cheaply. She hated the weekends with any idle time. Told me that staying busy is healthy."

"Brian likes helping you."

"You don't mind, do you?"

"No. I know you're watching him. He told me how you showed him what to do, then stood right there while he did it."

"I had to. He's too young to be doing it by himself, but I let him do enough to let him think he is."

"You've made him feel important."

"I've never known a youngster who took to something that

fast. Though I have to admit, I haven't known many children either. None really."

"Could have fooled me. You're a natural with them."

"Really?"

"Judging by Brian's glowing praises, yes. Have you finished the bed yet?"

"It's drying. Want to see it?"

Logan trailed after her as they went up the stairs.

In the back bedroom, she showed him the finished bed. It glowed like warm honey.

"Your bruises," he said. "They're gone."

She nodded. All the way up the stairs, she was conscious of him behind her. The way he looked at her now, she knew he was thinking about the kiss they'd just shared downstairs too.

Nervous, she picked up the photo of her dad and his mother. "I found this. My father was born in this bed."

Logan took the picture, looked at it, then at the bed. "You're right. That's Vera." Now he took a good look at the bed and back at the photo again. He whistled. "You've done a remarkable job. It looks brand new, just like in the photo. I wouldn't have had any idea that oak had been beneath that dark varnish."

"You knew Vera? She died the winter before my summer stay."

"No, I arrived shortly before you did, but everyone spoke kindly of her. She was well-known for her apple cobbler."

Charlene grinned. "I can't imagine why."

Logan grinned back. "I can't either. How are you at making

151

apple cobbler?"

"I don't know."

"I'll accept the responsibility of being your guinea pig providing you use Vera's recipe."

"If I can find it."

"I have faith in you." He handed back the photo. "Have you ever thought of having a family, Charlene?"

"On occasion. More so lately, mostly because I've had more time to think about my life." She smiled. "Plus, getting to know Brian. Yes, I'd like to have a family someday."

"What about your career?"

"Whoever I married would have to understand what I do is important to me. Few men enjoy being second banana, though."

"Sounds like you speak from experience."

"I do. Jealousy in any form creates a terrible barrier in a relationship."

"You're right. Speaking of family... earlier Brian forgot to invite you to come with us Saturday to Cornwell's."

"Cornwell's?"

"A restaurant well-known for its turkey sandwiches and turkey dinners."

"Sounds interesting."

* * * * *

The next morning, Charlene opened the door to let Cat out and found Jim Mulberry stacking boxes on her porch.

"These came for you," he said.

Looking at the return addresses, Charlene saw both the

Maestro's handwriting and Mike, who had sent her belongings. But, what had the Maestro sent her?

Once Jim left, she realized he'd done her a favor by bringing the boxes to the house. When he had asked if he could bring them inside, she had said yes. If she wasn't careful, she could get used to these small-town perks. Though she'd had some concern when she saw him looking around when bringing in the first box. That might not have been the smartest thing to do since she didn't know him that well.

After he left, she started opening the boxes. Inside one, she found the Maestro had sent her sheet music for next year's symphonies. In his own subtle way, he was asking her if she'd play and by sending her the music, she'd get her pick of dates.

* * * * *

Saturday arrived clear, sunny, and cold, reminding Charlene of the approaching winter season.

She loved the early mornings like this, the wisps of fog, dew heavy on the grass. From the kitchen window, she saw Cat lumber through the hundred-year-old lilac bushes and move toward the house. He'd be scratching at the door in a moment. Watching him move so slowly, she realized his arthritis was getting worse. She needed to take him to the vet. Monday she'd call.

She let Cat in, then she stood in the door, taking in the brilliant color in the trees. Overnight the leaves had changed. She could smell smoke in the air. Someone was burning leaves.

A cold gust of wind blew through the door. She shivered, then shut it.

She had a few hours of work ahead of her before Logan and Brian were due to pick her up.

* * * * *

Charlene glanced at the sign, did a double take, and laughed.

"What's so funny?" Brian asked.

He sat in the back, behind Logan, in a booster seat. Logan had insisted on driving the pickup truck. Charlene thought the car would have been more comfortable but Logan was determined.

"The sign said we were entering *Turkeyville*."

"We are."

"Does anyone live here?"

"There's a handful of houses, but basically it's the owners and their families."

A huge red barn came into sight. Across the street from it was a parking lot, cordoned off by a wooden fence. A white framed house stood in front of a L-shaped commercial looking building. "Which one is the restaurant?" she asked.

"That building," Logan said, pointing to the L-shaped one. Then he pointed to the house. "That's where the senior Cornwell's lived."

"All of that is the restaurant?"

"Not quite."

"You'll find out." Brian hurried her out of the vehicle now that Logan had parked it, and ran ahead of them.

While they ate, Charlene gazed at the antiques that filled walls, the old player piano that stood in the corner. Next to it stood a full-sized wooden Indian like the ones that use to sit outside general stores years and years ago.

"Would you believe this started as a small family restaurant," Logan asked.

"No."

"Now people come from all over. Bus loads from Indiana, Ohio, and Illinois."

After they ate, Brian pulled them into the Ice Cream Shoppe and Candy Store with Logan promising they'd stop back before going home.

Then Logan took her into the back wing where she browsed through candles, placemats, quilts, lace tablecloths, stationery, mugs, figurines, hats, and fudge.

"You haven't seen the best yet," he said, his eyes twinkling.

With Brian tugging on her good hand, and with Logan at her elbow, they led her across the street to the red barn. As they stepped through the huge door, Brian said. "This reminds me of Charlie's house."

Charlene's eyes widened at the sight of an entire barn filled with antiques. She turned her gaze to Logan.

"You should see your face. It's the same look Brian has when he comes downstairs Christmas Day and gets his first look at the tree."

"It is a little bit like Christmas," she admitted.

Charlene was very much aware of Logan shadowing her for the next half an hour, close enough to be nearby if she needed him, but not close enough to make her think he was hovering. She stopped at a free-standing oak mirror. She had almost missed it as it'd been hidden behind a high-boy.

"It's beautiful," she said, then sighed. "I've been looking a long time for a mirror like this. It's heavy; that means it's solid wood. And, the mirror is in mint condition."

"Then buy it."

"I can't," she sighed. With all the furniture I'm trying to get rid of, plus the money I'm trying to earn, it wouldn't make sense to make a purchase now."

"But, you said you've been wanting it for a long time."

"I have," she said with another sigh, turning. She took a step away from it.

Logan grabbed her arm and stopped her. "How can you walk away? Aren't you even curious to find out how much it is?"

"Whatever it is, it'll be too much."

"Wait here."

Before she could respond, he was gone. She watched him approach a clerk, and then, Brian demanded her attention. He had found an old toy and wanted to know how it worked.

Minutes later Logan returned. "It's yours."

"How much?"

"Fifty dollars."

Charlene gasped. "You're kidding?! That's a steal. Why is the price so low?"

"You're getting it for not much more than she paid for it."

"But that's ridiculous. Why would she do that?"

"Because I did some remodeling for her last year. At the

time, she told me to pick out a piece of furniture and it was mine at cost. I didn't then, but I am now."

She hesitated. It didn't feel right.

He looked at her and lowered his voice so only she could hear him. "I know you want it. You've got lust in your eyes."

"I do not," she quipped.

Logan bent over so he was even closer. "Trust me, it's lust."

Her face warmed. It was disturbing how easily Logan could read her thoughts these days. It could come back to haunt her.

She looked back at the mirror. Logan had taped a "SOLD" sign on it.

"Do we get to take it home with us now or do we have to come back after it?" she asked.

"Surely you jest. I couldn't leave this here, having you drool like a kid with her nose pressed against the candy store window. We take it with us now. Why do you think I brought the pickup? I had an idea you might find something."

She stood on tiptoes and kissed his cheek. "Thank you."

He smiled down at her. "You're welcome."

At every turn, Logan surprised her. She'd known him only a short time, yet her feelings for him were intense. She couldn't deny them any longer. Every day, every hour since that first meeting in Norton's office, she'd been determined not to think about her new partner, her neighbor. His absence from her side only fueled her imagination more.

She liked the way he teased her. The way he looked at her. The way he adored Brian. The way he looked at her now.

It was easy to love Logan. And Brian.

The realization hit her hard. She loved Logan, loved them both.

The thought took her breath away. As she stared at the two of them now, their heads together as they were involved in a deep discussion about a pea sheller that Brian had found and asked how it operated, Charlene wondered how she would ever be able to return to her former life without them.

"Are you ready?"

She blinked at the sound of Logan's voice, then nodded.

"Are you okay, Charlene? You look pale."

Charlene cleared her thoughts and smiled brightly. "I'm fine. What could be wrong? I just bought myself something I've always wanted." And will have to walk away one day from that which I never believed I would ever find, she thought.

A short time later, Charlene stood on the porch and waved good-bye as Brian and Logan went back to the truck. They'd brought the mirror into the house, but Charlene had them leave it downstairs for now. She'd have Logan move it upstairs later, after the room was finished. She was only half done and didn't want him to see it yet. She wanted to surprise him. He'd be seeing it soon enough.

* * * * *

Monday morning, Charlene arrived at the salesroom and found the parking lot full. Women were unloading the trunks of their cars, carrying armloads of stuff into the salesroom.

Charlene entered through the front door just as Logan

entered through the back room. He took one look around, his eyes widened, then seeing her, he came over and grabbed her arm, pulling her out of the traffic.

"It looks like an ant farm in here," he exclaimed, his voice a low rumble only she could hear. "What's going on?"

Charlene glanced around. Josie had already taken some crates, turned them on their sides and was displaying some of the items that had been brought in first thing. But now, she helped the women just stack the goods in a corner. Charlene figured she and Josie would set it all up later.

"Looks like our crafts have arrived."

One of the women came up to them. Logan released Charlene.

"Mrs. Murphy," he said. "Something I can help you with?"

"Logan Taylor, I can't tell you how much this means to me. My daughter's been telling me for years I ought to sell my quilts. I make more than we could ever possibly use. You're a godsend. Dad and I haven't had a vacation in years, not while putting all our youngsters through college. You've given us hope that we'll be able to. Even if it's nothing more than a weekend at Lake Michigan. Now, we won't have to wait another three years to take that vacation. Thank you."

Minutes later everyone was gone.

"My goodness," Josie said. "Are we in Oz now?"

Logan chuckled. "Not quite, but by the looks of it, you two get to clean up the aftermath of the tornado that just blew through here. Hope the two of you know what you're doing. Oh, Charlene, do you mind if I go to the house and take a look at your chimney and furnace? I need to take care of it before I forget again and while it's still daylight."

"Sure." Charlene dug in her purse for her key.

"That's okay," he said. "I've got my own key. See you later, ladies."

He had his own key? She didn't know that. That explained how he got into the house the night he'd found her in the attic, And the night he caught her when she fell from the footstool. She'd just assumed she'd forgotten to lock the door.

"Charlene? Where do you think we ought to display the quilts? On a line or a rack?"

Charlene turned back to Josie, and spent the rest of the morning arranging everything.

* * * * *

"Cat didn't come when I called him," Brian told Charlene.

By the time Charlene got home, it was four o'clock and Logan was gone. There were signs that he'd been here, though. He had left a note, saying he let Cat out. The weeds that had surrounded the outside door that led to the basement were gone and she'd seen an old furnace filter—disgustingly dirty—leaning against the trash can. Then Brian had arrived and was telling her Cat wasn't behaving.

"He didn't?" she said. "That's funny. He usually comes when you call. I wonder if he knows I've called the vet, and that he and I are going to go see him tomorrow. Call him again."

Brian returned, concern on his face. "I think you better call him, too. He's probably used to your voice now."

"Oh, you know Cat. He'll come. He's just slow." She studied Brian's worried face. "All right. Let me get my coat. And make sure you fasten yours up. It's getting colder outside."

They walked around the yard, calling Cat.

He didn't come.

Charlene frowned. She didn't know much about animals, but this wasn't normal for Cat. He was a creature of habit. He slept in her lap anytime she was sitting down, slept at the foot of the bed on her feet at night, scratched to go out, and meowed when he was ready to come in.

Though lately, he hadn't been leaving the house much and when he did, he wasn't gone long.

She used to watch him from the windows, stalking prey and occasionally bringing something to the door, meowing noisily until she came to the door, appreciating the gift he'd brought her.

Now that she thought about it, she hadn't seen him outside hunting for the last couple days. It was as if he'd suddenly lost interest.

They circled the yard a third time. "Dad says Cat is real old. He might never come back."

"Never come back?" She was aghast to think that an animal would wander off and get lost.

"We had a dog die. Dad said he was old and wanted to die alone. He found Red in the corner of the barn. We buried him in the back yard. Just like a real funeral. I've never been to one, but that's what Dad said they're like."

It was incredulous to Charlene, how their roles had just reversed. Brian sounded like the all-knowing adult and she the frightened young child.

"We'll find him," she said.

Moments later they did.

Cat lay among the lilac bushes, his coloring blending in with the leaves and twigs.

Charlene called out to Cat. He didn't move. She stood at the edge of the bushes, fearful.

"I'll get him," Brian said. He ducked down and started moving toward the animal.

Charlene put a hand on his shoulder, stopping him, her gaze still fastened on Cat. "No, let me." If anything was wrong, she didn't want Brian to discover it.

Bending over, holding her broken arm close to her chest, she went through the brush, pushing it aside with her other arm. In the center of the lilacs, she stood over Cat. His eyes were closed, but he looked funny.

Too still.

Gingerly she reached a hand out. Just an inch from his body, she stopped. Her heart hammered. *Please, don't let it be*, she thought.

She touched him.

Then drew her hand back quickly.

He was dead.

"Oh, Cat," she whispered. Tears formed in her eyes. She'd never seen an animal die before.

"Is he dead?" Brian asked.

"Yes," she finally said. She had to tell him the truth.

"I'll be right back," he said, turned and ran.

She called after him. "Brian! Wait!"

He ignored her, disappearing into the hedges. She sank down onto the ground. Leaves crunched beneath her. She needed to go after him.

Looking back at Cat, she bit her lip. Tears slid down her face. She couldn't carry him out, not with one hand. She couldn't leave him either.

She petted him, tears filling her eyes. She sniffed. "Why did you have to die?"

Leaves rustled.

"Charlene?"

Bent over, Logan came into the lilacs.

"Oh, Logan. Cat died." The tears spilled down her cheeks. "Brian called me."

Seconds later he was beside her and gathered her into his arms. She cried against his shirt, grateful for his strength and his low soothing voice.

"Ssshh," he said, smoothing her hair, pulling leaves from the dark strands.

"It's so sad. He died all alone. No one was with him. I should have been there for him."

"You were."

"No, I wasn't. He was out here. All alone. Brian spent more time with him than I did. *You* spent more time with him than I did."

She sniffled and ran her hand under her nose. Logan moved onto one hip and extracted something from his pocket. He pushed a handkerchief into her hand. Gripping it, she wiped her nose, then crushed it in her hand and grabbed a handful of his shirt. "I should have left New York more often and visited him."

"Cat?"

"No Gramps. I miss him."

"I miss him, too."

"What was he like? It's been so long since I had seen him. What was Gramps really like?"

"He was like you. Or rather, you're like him. He was stubborn. He cared about people, the community. He cared about the past—"

"Is that why he saved everything?"

"Possibly."

"Did you like working for him?"

"I never thought about it. But, yeah, I guess I did. He was always fair. Always willing to give me a chance. I remember the time I thought we should make our own crates. At first, he argued with me that it was cheaper to order them. I disagreed. So, he collected enough material for me to make a couple dozen crates. After I'd built them, he told me to total up the cost of the equipment, plus my wages involved. Among other things, I learned about wage expenses employers have to pay. That and how wrong I was. I listened to him more carefully after that. I didn't always agree, but I listened."

"What about your grandfather? Was he anything like

Charlie?"

"In some ways. But where Charlie acted younger than his age, Granddad acted older. He was sadder too."

"When did he die?"

"Just before I graduated from high school. If it weren't for that old man, I never would have completed high school. Especially that last year. After he died, I was ready to quit right then. But his words kept coming back to haunt me. *Make me proud* he always used to tell me. *Do the best you possibly can.*"

"Mother was the same way," Charlene said. "She was always striving for me to do what I wanted but to do it well."

"Let's go inside, Charlene. It's cold out here."

"What about Cat?" She couldn't stop looking at Cat. She sighed, determined not to cry again. Positive she wouldn't.

One lone tear slid down her cheek proving her wrong.

"I'll take him up to the house."

"No, we need to bury him."

"Let me call Hannah and Brian. He said he wanted to help bury Cat."

Inside, Logan dialed his number. She listened to him telling Brian that she was fine. Yes, they were ready for a funeral. And yes, if he wanted to bring it, they'd use it.

Logan hung up the phone.

"Use what?" she asked.

"A box. I'll go dig a hole. Any particular place you want him buried?"

"Somewhere near the lilacs, I think."

Setting water on to boil, Charlene spooned several teaspoons of a hot chocolate mix into a mug. She didn't really want the drink, but it gave her something to do. The kettle whistled. Brian entered the kitchen, a box under his arm. She turned the kettle off.

"I brought a box." He set it on the corner of the table. "It's my special box."

Charlene sat down. "Thank you, Brian. Special? How is it special?"

Brian sidled up beside Charlene, and she pulled him into her lap. "It was for my treasures. All the special things I wanted to keep."

"I think you're special."

Logan entered the kitchen. The sight of Brian sitting in Charlene's lap stopped him cold at the door. He'd heard Brian rave about Charlene, but he'd never really seen the two of them together... alone. It was obvious she cared about him. Charlene reached up and moved Brian's hair out of his face and listened intently while his son told her something. Then, she hugged him and kissed him on the cheek. Brian lit up, just as any boy his age would look at his own mother, Logan imagined. If only he could give Brian a mother.

Just then Charlene looked up, her brown eyes misty and soft.

Logan moved into the kitchen. "Did you bring the box, son?"

Charlene let go of Brian. He slid off her lap, grabbed the box, and went up to his dad. "Right here, Dad. Is it time?"

"It's time."

Hand-in-hand, with Brian in the middle, they went to the backyard. Charlene looked around. "Logan, I don't see where you've dug—"

"In the lilacs, where he died," Logan said. He parted the branches giving Brian and Charlene clear access to the center of the tall bushes. In the center, where they stood, was a foot-deep freshly dug hole.

Logan handed the box to Brian. Brian stooped, laid the box next to Cat, opened the box and scooped up several small handfuls of leaves, lining the box. Finished, Brian stood again, and tucked his small hand into hers.

Charlene blinked back tears as Logan gently lifted Cat into the box. Sprinkling a few more leaves on top of Cat, Logan put the cover on. Carefully, he placed the box into the hole. Picking up the shovel, Logan scooped up some dirt, prepared to toss it into the hole.

He froze hearing Brian's voice.

"Aren't we going to say anything?"

"Sure son." He set the shovel down. Logan hesitated, then began. "We'll never forget Cat. He wasn't the best-looking animal, but what he lacked in looks, he made up in charm. Cat loved everyone he encountered. Rescued when he was just a kitten, he lived a good life. We'll miss him."

In a semicircle, the three of them stood looking down at the sealed box.

"He was a good cat," Brian said, solemnly.

Logan put a hand on Brian's shoulder and squeezed. For Charlene, the ground became bleary. She looked up at Logan. He at her.

"The best," she said, and a tear trickled down her cheek. Dashing it away, she looked down at Brian. He was looking up at the clouds through the bare branches. "What is it, Brian?" she asked.

"Do animals go to heaven?"

She glanced back at Logan. He was as surprised as she was at the question. "I don't know," she answered.

Logan knelt down to his son. "They have their own special heaven."

"They do?"

"I'm sure of it. None of us really knows what heaven is like."

"Do you think Cat's happy?" Brian asked.

"Most definitely."

Brian turned to her. "I'm hungry."

She smiled and ruffled his hair. "We've got those cookies we made the other day."

"Chocolate chip! Oh boy." He was gone, just a blur of color as he disappeared into the house.

"You go on ahead, too," Logan told her. "I'll finish up here."

"Thank you. For everything. The funeral. The words. Everything."

He looked at the hole, the box waiting to be covered, then finally at her. "It was nothing."

She put a hand on his forearm. "Yes, it was. You made Cat's

death—his funeral—special."

* * * * *

From the kitchen window, Charlene watched Logan lean the shovel against the house, then wipe his brow with his shirt sleeve. Despite the cold air, he carried his jacket.

As she studied his profile, she saw the strength in his face, the same strength reflected in his body as he bent over and rinsed his hands at the spigot. Strength, she realized, that she'd come to depend on.

Logan rose, shaking his wet hands. Drops of water glistened in the sun as they fell to the ground. Spotting her in the window, Logan smiled and winked.

She smiled.

She heard his boots stomp on the threshold.

"What's this?" he asked, seeing Charlene making sandwiches.

"Supper. Hannah called saying since Brian was over here, she wanted to run to the store. I told her to take her time, that I'd feed him dinner, but she said something about getting right back and putting her feet up. You're invited to stay, too."

"Where's Brian?"

"Washing his hands in the bathroom." She smiled. "Afterward, he'll stop and visit with the birds. He has a routine. Or rather, the three of them have a routine."

"And, I see you've got it down pat."

She reached for Brian's glass, filling it with milk. "Hungry?"

"Starving."

At the husky tone of his voice, she glanced at him. His gaze was fastened on her. A treacherous flame engulfed her as she held the milk in her hand.

"I'll take a glass of that, too." Their fingers touched as he took the glass, and for just a few seconds, he held her hand captive before letting her go, hearing Brian.

He entered the room. "After supper, can I help work on the bed?"

"Believe it or not, it's all done. Now, it has to be assembled."

"I could help with that."

"No, Sport," Logan said. "By the time we're done with dinner, Hannah will be back. You'll need to go home. I don't like Hannah being left alone too long these days."

Later Brian said, "Okay. I'm done now." He looked to Charlene. "May I take some cookies with me?"

"Sure. Take a few for Hannah, too."

Minutes later, he left. As was her habit, she went to the window and watched until he disappeared in the shrubbery. Logan came and stood behind her. "He's a sweetie, Logan. You're lucky to have him."

"I know. If you want, I can help you assemble the bed," he suggested.

To Charlene, the air crackled with electricity. "Now?"

"No time like the present, but let me go check the orchard first and then I'll be back later. I want to make sure everything got closed, plus check on that one thermometer that was giving us a problem. Or will that be too late?"

"No. Actually, that'll work out fine." There were a couple more things she needed to do before Logan saw the room.

Logan left and Charlene went back to the kitchen to put away the refrigerated foods before they spoiled. She would have to come back later to clean up the kitchen. Right now, she wanted to get upstairs.

Chapter 9

"Is this where you want it?"

Logan set the mirror down. He couldn't keep his gaze off Charlene. She had changed into black skin-tight leggings and wore a red sweatshirt that ended just where things got interesting. She had legs that men dreamed of and other women wished they had.

After he'd gone to the orchard, closing everything up, then went home to check up on Hannah and Brian, only to find both of them cozied up in front of the TV with a movie and popcorn and Hannah's assurance it was okay to go help Charlene, he'd left his truck at home and came in through the backyard. He felt like he was sneaking in and for the life of him he couldn't shake the feeling or understand it.

He stepped back, then blinked. This wasn't the same room he'd been in just a week ago. The walls were soft peach in color. A potted fern in a wicker stand stood in front of a window. Lace curtains, clean and wrinkle free hung from the windows. The excess furniture was gone.

"I found the curtains in the attic," she told him. "Most needed only minor repairs, mostly to the hems and one pair was beyond help, but otherwise there are enough for all the upstairs windows. I'd like to add some shades, though, for privacy."

"Is the lace antique?"

"I'm pretty sure it is. I thought I'd use the curtains while I was here, though I can't imagine you'd want anything this delicate hanging for your windows."

"It suits you. Every woman needs to have a bedroom she feels comfortable in."

"But, what about her husband? Shouldn't a bedroom reflect his tastes too?"

"That's why we have dens," he said with a grin. "How did you get the furniture moved? When did you have time to paint the walls? You've been at the orchard late mornings and several hours in the afternoons. I know Brian spends the rest of the afternoons with you. Hannah thanks you for that, by the way. Me too. I worry about her."

"Josie and her boyfriend helped with the furniture, and I've been working on it at night." Especially when she couldn't sleep. "Once I found the bed, I knew I had to put it in the same room where it once belonged."

"I thought I was going to do the painting."

"I was anxious to get the room done. Once I got the hang of using the roller with one hand, it wasn't difficult. The man at the hardware store said you had an account there. Was that all right?"

"Yeah, that's fine. You know, had you asked me if I wanted this in peach, I would have said no."

"Oh, Logan. I'm sorry. I thought once you saw it, you'd like it. It's just when I saw that color and it was on sale—"

"Charlene, it's okay. I like it. The room will really be finished, though, once the floor has been sanded."

"Are you going to keep the floors bare?"

"I don't know. Guess I haven't thought about it." He paused for a second. "What do you recommend?"

"Personally, I like wooden floors. With this bed, and a few throw rugs, it'll look great, but it depends on what look you want."

"Lots of time to decide that." Logan clapped his hands together. "For now, we've got a bed to move. But first, we better get this one out of here."

"Let me strip the sheets off."

She gathered the sheets and blanket to her chest.

He moved forward to help her. "Let me take that," he said. Reaching around the bundle to grasp it, his hand brushed her breast. They both froze.

Their gaze met across the top of the bedding. A faint tinge of color stained her cheeks.

"I've got it," he said, huskily.

He watched her gulp, nod her head, and let go. Her hand which was encased between the bedclothes and his chest slid down his belly.

His muscles grew taut, and he sucked in air at her touch. She turned, grabbed the pillows, and tossed them on top of the bedding that he had thrown onto the floor, out of the way.

Logan leaned the mattress against the wall, then went for the box spring, lifting it off the bed, and leaned it against the mattress. He then removed the old metal frame, taking it out into the hall. Piece by piece, he brought in the old wooden bed. Logan placed the footboard in position instructing her to stand behind it, while he attached the frame.

His concentration was total as he held the corners together and picked up the screwdriver. Palming it, the muscles in his forearm bunched as he worked the tool, twisting the screws into place.

Then, finally, the slats were in place. The frame assembled, they moved it into its final position.

"What do you think?" he asked.

"It looks wonderful."

"It'll look even better when the springs and mattress are in place. Shall we?"

The whole time he'd been putting the frame together visions of Charlene in the bed had entered his mind. It was all he could do to concentrate on what he was doing with the tools in his hands and not let one slip and mar her refinishing job or take a chunk of skin out of his hand.

One-handed, Charlene helped Logan with the box springs as best she could. The mattress was a little more difficult, but finally the bed was together.

He reached for the bedding on the floor, Charlene stopped him by saying, "Let me get some clean sheets."

Out in the hall, opening the linen closet, Charlene let her forehead rest against one of the shelves. *Good Lord*, she thought. Any minute now she expected fireworks to go off. Or thunder to follow the bolts of electricity that occurred between them. The air practically sizzled in there.

Never had she experienced such sensations as she had in the last few moments. Every time his hand brushed against her, her heart skipped a beat.

Logan spoke from behind her.

"Tired?" he asked her.

She straightened. "No... no... not at all."

He reached around her, his arms circling her, and he grabbed a set of sheets. "These okay?"

She nodded. He could have asked if nettles were okay and she would have said yes.

Following him into the bedroom, she watched has he snapped open the bottom sheet. It floated down until it lay on the mattress. The air crackled with heat and electricity.

Her palms sweaty, her heartbeat felt erratic. Weak-kneed, she went to the other side of the bed and pulled the sheet over the headboard corner. Logan mimicked her motions. They stared at each other as they both moved to the foot of the bed and tucked the other corners into position.

Still staring at her, he grabbed the flat sheet on one edge and shook it out. She could only watch. He disappeared from view, then she saw him watching her from beneath the sheet, just before he disappeared behind the material again as the sheet ballooned out and floated down, and then he was in view again.

He let go and moved purposefully around the bed coming around the far corner, then her corner. His gaze was intense and steady and she could see the desire in his eyes was as raw as the desire she felt in her body. She turned to meet him.

The air was so thick, she could hardly breathe. But breathe she did, and when she did, it was to inhale the smell of him. She closed her eyes against the heady aroma. She felt his arms slip around her, and she stepped into his embrace.

"Logan," she whispered.

"You feel it, too." He nuzzled her neck.

She felt the pins in her hair slide out slowly. Fingers threaded through her hair, massaging her scalp. Logan pulled back, his fingers fanning her hair out around her head.

"I've been wanting to do that for a long time. I feel as if I'm the first to do that."

"You are," she whispered.

He kissed her, and shivers of delight swept over her. She was putty in his hands. For the first time ever, she wanted to forget her vow of chastity until marriage.

He kissed her again, this time quickly and efficiently, but before his mouth left hers, his teeth pulled gently on her lower lip. A slow smile curved her mouth as she watched him back away.

"I've got to go before we do something that we might regret." He kissed her on the forehead, then left.

She sighed, wishing he wouldn't leave but knowing he had to.

Chapter 10

Throughout the next couple weeks, Logan and she shared many special moments. Like when Logan got her into the freezer on the pretense of getting produce for customers, and delayed her by kissing her senseless.

The salesroom stayed busy and she was glad. Logan was too. It looked like they'd have a good season.

Charlene thought about how her days were hectic but happy as she pulled into Logan's driveway. His house resembled hers only it was smaller, and it looked as if it had been recently painted. Brian, at the window, waved to her and the curtain fell into place.

She was going to Marshall to have her cast removed and Brian was going with her. It was hard to believe six weeks had flown by this quickly.

The front door opened and Brian burst out the door as if he'd been shot out of a cannon. Hannah stood at the door and waved to Charlene. She waved back. Hannah's due date was yesterday. Logan had told Charlene he didn't expect Hannah to continue watching Brian, but Hannah had been insistent, saying she needed to stay busy or she'd go crazy. This was Hannah's first child, but she didn't appear anxious like other first-time mothers. Hannah had told Charlene that she had half a dozen nieces and nephews and had assisted two of her sisters during the birth of three of their children.

Charlene laughed at the miniature dynamo, as he attempted unsuccessfully to open the car door. She got out and opened the back door for him.

An hour later, she sat on a low stool, her arm resting on Dr. Hunter's examining table. He held a saw-like instrument above her cast. He'd already taken an x-ray.

Brian, who had been sitting in the corner quietly until now, blurted, "Aren't you afraid it's going to hurt, Charlene?"

"She shouldn't be," Dr. Hunter explained. "The saw stops when it reaches skin."

"It does?"

At Brian's incredulous response, the doctor and she exchanged a grin.

"Would you like a closer look?" he asked him.

Brian nodded enthusiastically. Dr. Hunter laid the instrument down, and pulled a chair opposite Charlene.

"Over here," he said, indicating the chair to the small boy. "But don't get too close."

Brian watched wide-eyed as the saw bit into the cast, small

pieces of plaster flying everywhere.

At last the cast was cut through. Dr. Hunter turned the machine off, set it aside and inserted his thumbs into the crack. Seconds later, the cast lay open and her arm was free.

"Wow!" Brian exclaimed. "Can I have it?"

Dr. Hunter looked at her questioningly, and she nodded.

"Sure," he said, handing the cast to the boy.

Charlene flexed her fingers and wrist.

"It's going to take time to get the muscles back in proper working order," he told her after he'd inspected her arm. "Carry a golf or tennis ball, squeezing it every chance you get. It'll speed up the recovery, help strengthen your muscles."

He walked them to the door that would lead them back to the reception area. "If that arm gives you any trouble, don't hesitate to give me a call. Bye, Brian."

"Bye, Doc. Thanks!"

They walked downtown and stopped at the Stagecoach Inn, a famous Marshall landmark for lunch. Having noticed the Halloween decorations in the storefronts, Charlene asked Brian, "What are you going to be for Halloween?"

"A birthday boy."

"How do you dress for that?"

"Regular clothes."

Charlene frowned. "When is your birthday?"

"Halloween."

"Don't you go trick-or-treating?"

"No. We have cake and ice cream, but first we go to my

favorite restaurant."

She had an idea.

* * * * *

After her appointment, she drove to the orchard since Logan had asked her to.

Brian spotted him immediately out in the orchard. The car had barely stopped when Brian had the door open and dashed off to his dad.

Logan, hearing Brian calling out to him, turned and opened his arms, catching Brian and spinning him around. The little boy laughed, then when set down spun around in a dizzying circle.

Just as she shut her car door, a car pulled up alongside of hers. The driver rolled down his window and stuck a cardboard tube out his window.

"Can you give this to Logan Taylor?" he asked.

"Sure." She took the tube eyeing it quizzingly. "What is it?"

"Some new plans he ordered." The car was already backing up. "Thanks!" Then, he drove off.

Charlene wondered what they were. Certainly not of the building. Logan would have talked to her about it. Wouldn't he?

Brian, pulling Logan behind him, joined her in the parking lot. Charlene pasted a smile on her face as she handed the tube for Logan.

"That was just dropped off for you."

"Thanks, I've been expecting it."

"Charlene," Brian said. "Show dad your arm."

Logan took her newly bared arm in his hand and ran his

hand back and forth on her skin. "How does the arm feel?"

"Weightless. It's hard to get used to, and I keep forgetting I can use my left hand now."

"Brian told me already about the cast being cut off. And that he has it?"

Charlene nodded. "A souvenir."

"And what's this about a costume?"

"I wanted to talk to you about that. Halloween is in two days and Brian said he's never been trick-or-treating."

"I've never really had time to take him. Up until now, he's been too young."

"Well, I want you and Brian to come to my Halloween party. Just a small party. To celebrate my freedom, too," she said holding up her arm. "I was thinking of inviting Hannah and Josie too. And then afterward—"

"Afterward?" Logan eyes widened with anticipation.

"Afterward, we'll go trick-or-treating."

"You and Brian can go."

"Don't you want to go?" she asked. Logan didn't answer. "What's the matter?" she continued. "Did you throw eggs or steal someone's pumpkin the last time you trick-or-treated and got caught?"

"No. It's just never been a holiday I celebrated growing up. We didn't have money for costumes. I guess that's why I never cared for the holiday. For class parties, I just used an old sheet and dressed as a ghost. Didn't take any work on my part, and the teachers didn't have to feel sorry for me."

"This year is going to be different. You'll see. You'll enjoy it. And don't worry about a costume. I've got something that will fit you just fine."

"I've got to wear a costume?"

"If you want your treats afterward you do."

Logan laughed. "All right, you win. You know where my weak spot is."

"Chocolate, right?" she teased.

* * * * *

Two nights later, Charlene, Brian, and Logan exited her front door for a night of trick-or-treating. Josie, her boyfriend, and Hannah had been there for Charlene's party and had already left for other evening events.

"Wait a minute, Logan. Your patch is still up." She reached up and pulled the black eye patch in place. "There. Much better."

"I feel ridiculous," Logan said.

"You look good, Dad." Brian said.

"You're a true rake of a pirate," Charlene added.

"This earring hurts. How do you woman wear them?"

"We get used to them."

"I like your outfit better," he said.

"I like mine best of all," Brian exclaimed. He jumped in the air and landed, his knees bent, his sword in hand ready to do battle. "I'm an Avenger!"

Charlene blushed at the way Logan ogled her Scheherazade outfit, at her slightly exposed belly.

"Nice belly button," he added, for her ears only.

" Let's go," Brian said.

"What a party animal I'm raising," Logan quipped.

"Let me lock the door," Charlene said. She heard the phone ring. Charlene paused. "Let me go see who that is. I had called the Maestro earlier and he wasn't in. It might be him."

Seconds later, she returned to the porch. "It's for you, Logan. It's Alan. Says there's a problem."

Logan left her and Brian on the porch. A minute later Logan returned.

"Sorry guys. Trouble with the freezer again. I've got to go fix it, and it sounds like it'll be a couple hours. You two go on ahead. I'll meet you back here later."

"Aw, Dad," Brian said with obvious disappointment. "You're going to miss all the fun."

Logan hunkered down to Brian's eye level. "Yeah, I know, but it can't be helped. You take good care of Charlene, and then you can tell me all about it when you get back."

"Okay."

* * * * *

Back home, Charlene pulled into the driveway just as Logan pulled in.

Brian burst out of the car and ran toward his father. "Dad, Dad, look at all the candy I got. You want some?"

Logan bent and picked up Brian, and she listened to their discussion about which candy bar was the best as they all walked up to the porch and into the house.

"Anybody want some hot chocolate?" she asked.

They followed her down the hall to the kitchen. With her back to them, she took the kettle to the sink and turned on the tap water.

To Logan, she said, "If you start a fire, we can roast some marshmallows."

Logan left to start the fire with Brian following him.

Minutes later, she joined them, carrying a tray ladened with hot chocolate and marshmallows. Logan jumped up and took the tray from her and set it down. Charlene reached for the sticks she'd gathered earlier, the ends now sharpened to a fine point.

Brian eagerly stuck a marshmallow on the end of his and sat in front of the blazing fire. Logan showed him just where to hold the stick so it wouldn't burn to a crisp too fast.

"This has been the best night ever," he exclaimed, his eyes fastened on the marshmallow.

Logan looked at her from over the top of his son's head. "Thanks."

Charlene smiled. Love swelled through her, filling her heart to overflowing. With sudden clarity, she realized this was what she wanted for her life. A family, living in a small community...

What a change from when she'd first arrived. Before, she hadn't ever given a thought to having a family, now the thought occupied a lot of her time. She loved it here in Willow Junction and hated to think of the time she'd have to leave.

The leaves had turned color and were already dropping with more trees bare each morning. Soon, the landscape would be bleak against gray snow clouds, but she looked forward to it.

She knew, however, once she got back to New York, she'd be busy, but she'd never forget her time here. She had a sold-out year-long tour ahead of her, but after that she could return to Willow Junction from time to time. And do what?

It was foolish to think Logan would wait patiently for her. She couldn't ask him to either. So, where did that leave them? As much as she hated to admit it, their relationship was just a brief interlude. An intermission in their otherwise busy lives.

And then, there was Brian to think of. She looked his way. He had fallen asleep on the sofa.

Charlene got an afghan and covered him up. Then, she went to sit next to Logan on the floor in front of the fireplace. The marshmallow he roasted caught fire, and he pulled it out and blew the fire out. He offered it to her, but she shook her head.

She looked at Brian. "First time I've ever seen him worn out. "His energy is endless."

"A shame it's wasted on youth."

"Not all of it," Logan said, putting down his marshmallow and stick. "I've got some energy left. Okay, a little."

Charlene giggled as he drew her down among the pillows on the floor. "Oh, you are a pirate!"

"And I want to capture your treasures." He kissed her, then moved his mouth across her cheek to the sensitive spot on her neck that he knew would get a reaction from her. It did. She sighed and wrapped her arms around him.

They hugged for a minute, then they sat back up and continued roasting marshmallows with fire throwing light and shadow against their bodies.

"I heard you playing the piano when Brian and I arrived earlier. How's the arm?"

"It's going to take some work to get back up to speed. I was surprised how much it hurt after playing for just half an hour."

"It'll come. I hate to say it, but I think the party is over. It's been a long day."

Charlene agreed, looking over at the little boy sleeping on her sofa. "It's time to get him home and in bed."

She gave Logan a quick kiss.

"You're a hard woman to leave, Charlene Walker." He got to his feet and offered her his hand. She accepted and with a tug, she was on her feet, too. He stood, then wrapped his arms around her. "Marry me, Charlene." He couldn't believe he had just blurted that out, but now that he had, he was glad. He couldn't imagine life without her.

Startled, Charlene looked up at him. Did he just say what she thought she heard?

"Don't say anything now. Just think about it."

She was stunned. Did he have any idea what he was asking her? Had he forgotten her career, her other commitments? It would be like asking him to leave his home, his job, to come to New York.

A bolt of lightning lit up the outside. Thunder followed quickly.

Charlene jumped.

She took Brian's coat from Logan's fingers and put it on the boy while Logan held Brian's limp body against him.

She peered out the window. "Looks like we're in for a storm."

"I just hope the temperature doesn't drop."

They were talking as if he'd never asked her to marry him. Now, she wondered if he really had.

He continued. "Freezing rain would be disastrous for the orchard, at this point. There's still about a third of the crop on the trees. If we'd had better machinery, it would have all been picked by now."

Charlene could see he was more worried than he let on.

With Brian coated, Logan grabbed Brian's bag of candy. "Thanks again. You made tonight special for this little guy. For me, too."

"I enjoyed it, as well." She followed him to the door and turned on the porch light. She waited until Logan's headlights disappeared before shutting the door. A crack of lightning, closer this time, made her jump. She cringed waiting for the thunder, which followed quickly.

She went to the window and saw rain pelting the pane. Back in the parlor, she collected the dirty dishes and took them to the kitchen. The thermometer outside the window read thirty-five degrees.

As she got ready for bed, the rain continued to batter the roof. Taking one last look out the window, she noticed the yard appeared glossy.

Tucked warmly under the covers in bed, she thought about Logan and their relationship. It wasn't a simple matter of saying yes or no. There were so many other things they needed to talk about. Her career, her life in New York. Logan didn't strike her as a person who would welcome his girlfriend, let alone a wife, being away from home for long periods of time. No easy solution for a relationship came to mind.

The next morning, she woke up tired and restless, knowing she'd tossed and turned most of the night. Outside, the weather looked like she felt. Dark clouds threatened to spill more rain. The temperature gauge hovered at thirty-three degrees.

By afternoon it started raining again, only harder. By mid-afternoon it was dark as night and the sleet began.

Two hours later, the lights went out. Going to the window she saw the birch tree in the yard doubled over, the top of the tree touching the ground.

Logan called asking if she was all right, and she asked about the orchard. He told her there was nothing they could do but wait out the storm.

As the day passed, the temperature dropped another degree, but still the rain didn't change to snow. She fed the fire, grateful for the wood stacked outside the back door. Unable to work on the refinishing or to do any cleaning, she went to the piano, taking several candles with her.

Without any music in front of her, Charlene started playing. At first, her fingers were stiff, but quickly they warmed up. Half an hour into her playing, however, she felt her arm stiffening up until finally she just couldn't go on any longer.

Several times earlier she had tried to play, and each time she had reached this same painful wall and couldn't seem to get past it. It worried her, but then maybe she was expecting too much too soon.

For dinner, Charlene heated water for soup and hot chocolate at the fireplace.

Just as she set the kettle on, the telephone rang. It was Logan, and he was concerned about her. Not always able to get good cell phone reception here, she was glad for the landline. When the power went out, she still had a working phone, like now.

"I'm doing as well as can be expected. How's Hannah?"

"Miserable, especially since her husband was supposed to be home today, but he's stuck in Missouri somewhere because of this storm. It's wreaking havoc in several states."

"I thought he wouldn't be here until after the baby was born."

"He got an earlier leave, but just for a few days."

"Give her my best."

"I want your best, along with the rest of you," he growled.

* * * * *

Several hours later, Logan phoned again. "Can you come stay with Brian? Hannah's gone into labor. Bring a bag, you'll probably be spending the night. I'll come and get you—"

"No, no. Stay with Hannah and Brian. I'll be there in a few minutes."

Quickly, she covered the birds, packed an overnight bag, then bundled up against the raw weather. It took her ten minutes just to cross her yard. Her sneaker-clad feet threatened to slide in opposite directions every other step. Cleats would have been the best thing for this slippery surface, she thought, catching herself from falling for the umpteenth time.

When she finally reached the hedge, the sky released yet another flood. Before she'd gone ten yards, she was soaked and chilled. Now the rain stung as it hit her face. It was sleeting again.

The ice on the ground was even slicker now. Fearing she'd lose her footing and break her arm again, or worse a leg, she stopped. There had to be a better way to negotiate on the icy ground.

Awkwardly at first, Charlene found a rhythmic movement without lifting her feet off the ground. Seconds later she was at the porch. Logan was there, his hand out. She grabbed hold.

"You're soaked," he said, shutting the door behind them.

She shivered, her teeth chattering.

"Get in front of the fire right now. You need to get out of those clothes."

"They'll dry in front of the fire. All I brought was a nightgown and a toothbrush." She moved to the fireplace, glad for the heat. She tried unbuttoning her coat but couldn't as she started shivering more violently.

He unbuttoned her coat for her, removing it, and hanging it on a hook. He grabbed a blanket off the couch, handing it to her.

"Get these wet things off, and I'll find you something to wear."

When he returned, she was as close to the fire as she could possibly get, shaking uncontrollably, but still wearing most of her clothes.

Logan peeled off her sweatshirt, then had the hem of her T-shirt in his hands.

"No.... not... not... here."

"Honey, you're freezing cold. You can hardly talk."

"I'll... do it."

"Okay. I'll turn my back, but just long enough until you get this on." He handed her a T-shirt and navy-blue sweater and sweat pants.

Quickly, she stripped off her shirt and bra and pulled the dry T-shirt and sweater over her head. Then the pants. The sweater came to her knees, and the pants were huge, but by using the tie-cord at the waist, she kept them from sliding down. "All done."

Logan turned and started rubbing her arms, then her legs.

Gritting her teeth to keep them from chattering, she said, "Where's Brian?"

"He's out in the kitchen with Hannah. They're making hot chocolate."

"Her... her... contractions?" she chattered.

"We've still got time to get to the hospital."

Hannah and Brian entered the room.

Logan handed her a mug of hot chocolate. Brian, with great care, set a plate of crackers and cheese on a footstool. "I didn't drop one," he said grinning. Then he peered intently at Charlene. "You don't look blue."

Logan ruffled his hair. "That's because you didn't see her when she first came in."

Hannah had one hand at her back, the other rubbing her swollen belly.

"How are you feeling?" Charlene asked Hannah.

"Relieved now that the great event is about to happen. The contractions are about twenty minutes apart."

Hands wrapped around her mug, Charlene gulped at the liquid, grateful for the heat that slid down her throat.

Hannah groaned, her hands on her swollen belly.

"And time to go," Logan said.

Once Brian was seated on the sofa, Logan handed him a mug of hot chocolate half-filled.

"Be careful," Charlene told them. "It's real slippery."

Logan gave her a quick kiss.

She followed them to the door and watched as Logan guided Hannah to the car with painstakingly small steps. Just before he closed his door, he yelled, "I'll call as soon as I know anything."

Charlene nodded, and shut the door against the unrelenting sleet that poured out of the sky.

Going back to the living room, she sat next to Brian. "Well, kiddo. I guess it's just you and me. What are we going to do?"

"We could make brownies."

"The power's out."

"But our stove still works."

"It does?"

Sure enough, when they went to the kitchen, Charlene discovered the appliance was gas not electric and was working.

"Brownies it is," she announced.

As they mixed the batter, Brian asked, "How come you didn't bring the birds?"

"They would have gotten wet."

"Do they like being alone?"

"They have each other for company. They'll talk to each other."

"But, won't they get cold with no lecticity?"

"Electricity. No, they'll be all right. I covered them up. The room is warm because of the fire I had and the bricks will stay warm for a while. And I threw an extra covering over them.

Around eight, the phone rang. It was Logan calling to report Hannah had a baby girl and that he was going to stay at the hospital. The roads were too dangerous to travel.

* * * * *

When the sun rose the next morning, Charlene looked out the window. The sky was clear, her entire view sparkling as if coated in diamonds.

An inch-thick coating of ice covered everything. Limbs lay strewn about on the ground. The grass looked stiff, and flat surfaces looked smooth as glass.

Soon after, Logan arrived home. He folded her into his arms, kissing her.

"I'll feel better once I'm showered and changed," he told her. "And then, I'm going to the orchard, dropping Brian off at Fran Weddington's. She'll be watching him now."

"I don't mind watching him."

"But, I do. It's not your job. You've got your own work. Besides, you look beat. Didn't get any sleep, did you?"

She reached for her coat. She wanted to talk to him but now wasn't a good time what with everything that was happening.

"If you'll wait, I'll drive you home," he said.

"That's all right. I'll skate home. Now that I know how to do it. Go take care of Brian. I'll be all right."

He kissed her one more time. "Be careful."

Home safe, she checked on the birds first. Since the power hadn't been restored yet, she built another fire.

Upstairs, she stripped off Logan's clothes and changed into her own.

She longed to go to the orchard and check on the damage, but she was afraid to venture out. The roads would be dangerous. Better to stay home.

The longer she didn't hear from Logan, though, the more concerned she became. She called the orchard. Josie answered.

"The remaining crop has been destroyed."

"How's Logan taking it?"

"Bad. Here he is now."

"Wait... Josie?"

"It's me, Logan."

"Oh, Logan. I'm so sorry about the crop."

"It's not your fault."

"But, we could have harvested the entire crop."

"Charlene. It wasn't your fault. We couldn't find what we needed in time. When you deal in agriculture, the weather can be your enemy. This isn't the first time we've lost part of the crop, and it won't be the last. We're still in business, despite ourselves. I'll be over in about an hour. Is that okay with you?"

"Sure."

Charlene hung up the phone. She wrung her hands wondering how Logan was going to take what she would tell him.

* * * * *

"I can't marry you, Logan."

Logan had barely taken his coat off before asking her if she had an answer to his proposal. Now, the smile was gone from his face and he studied her intently.

"I see."

"Just not right now."

"That's letting me down easy, isn't it? Not right now. Don't you mean as in ever?"

Charlene gasped. "That's not what I said. Why are you being so harsh?"

"Harsh? I thought you felt the same way as I do."

"I do."

"Doesn't look like it from where I'm standing."

"Logan, my career is important to me."

"And a career of being a wife, mother, and owning an orchard isn't?"

"That's not what I said. I've got other commitments that I have to honor first."

"Charlene, you don't have to explain anything to me. You said no. I'm a big boy. I understand what the word means. If nothing else, I've learned to realized when a woman doesn't want me anymore."

He turned on his heel and left.

"Logan, wait!" But, he didn't. The door shut behind him. She wanted to tell him how she felt. Now, she had botched this all up by being so direct and up front with her first sentence. She should have worked her way up to it. No. He should have been more patient, hearing her out. What a mess.

He was wounded. Nothing she could have said would have made any sense. Even though his first wife had left him long ago, she had opened those scars in telling him she couldn't marry him. It wasn't that she didn't want to marry him. She did. She loved him, but she needed to be healed and debt-free first. Plus, having a long-distance relationship wouldn't work for him or for her, nor would it be fair to Brian.

She'd done the right thing in telling him no. Hadn't she cautioned herself in the beginning not to get involved with Logan? This was the culmination of those fears. Well, there was nothing she could do to change anything now.

* * * * *

In the weeks that followed, Charlene wished over and over that she could go back and change things. Change how involved she got with Logan, wishing they'd stayed just friends. But then, minutes later, she'd acknowledge that she wouldn't change a thing.

She'd found a man she loved. And, she had loved. It'd been the best experience of her life. She doubted she'd ever meet another man who could replace him, nor did she want anyone else to replace him. There was no way they could be together, not with her career and his inability to move around with her. He was landlocked to this community, to his son.

Though it was difficult, she continued to go to the orchard in the mornings. Every day that passed with Logan virtually ignoring her other than when it came to business put a strain on her nerves, but there was nothing she could do. She remained friendly, but Logan didn't want to be around her any more than he had to.

At one point, Josie asked her if anything was wrong, and Charlene told her she'd have to ask Logan.

"I did," Josie said. "Nearly lost my head, his roar was so violent."

They didn't discuss Logan after that.

Brian, however, was as gregarious as his father was reticent. And, he continued to visit her daily, mostly on the phone. A couple times a week, she'd pick him up from Fran's and bring him home with her. Logan would call so she could send Brian home through the shrubs. At times, she wondered if this was how divorced parents acted. Polite but nothing deeper. A brave face for the kids.

Brian chatted about how Logan had taken him to see Hannah and her baby. How Fran was making pumpkin pies to sell and how he was helping her, and what he and his dad did together at night. The boy was oblivious to the problems she and Logan were having, and Charlene was determined he wouldn't learn anything was wrong from her.

The more immediate problem, however, was her arm. Her

playing hadn't been improving.

Now, she sat waiting in one of the doctor's examining rooms.

Finally, the door opened.

"Trouble with the arm, Miss Walker?" The doctor shut the door.

After Charlene explained the problem, she watched as the doctor went through her file. Frowning, he looked up at her, sitting back in his chair. "Did your doctor in New York explain to you that there was a great likelihood that you wouldn't be able to go back to your career as a pianist?"

"Yes, but I didn't believe him. I thought he was just being a bit pessimistic. He usually is."

"Not in this case. I've looked at your x-rays, and from what you're describing, everything he said was true. Miss Walker, your injury was severe. It wasn't just a simple break. You damaged nerves. Repetitive action, such as playing the piano, puts a strain on those nerves. That's the pain you're feeling. I'm sorry."

Chapter 11

Stunned, Charlene could only sit there and stare at him.

He patted her hand. "I truly wish I had some better news for you."

Closing her file, he stood. "I wish you the best. If you have any other questions, please don't hesitate to call me."

She could barely get the words out. "Thank you, Doctor."

The minute the door shut behind him, tears fell. Looking up, she willed them to stop. Gritting her teeth, she made herself get up, leave the room, leave the office, and go across the parking lot to her car.

Her career was over.

Just like that. One moment of terrorism and her life was changed forever. She'd been made a victim twice.

Her first instinct was to run home and call the Maestro. Trouble was, he couldn't fix it either. Nor did she want to unload on him. He'd have enough problems to deal with once she told him she wouldn't be coming back to the orchestra next year as they had planned. Someone else would be taking her place permanently.

When Charlene turned off the ignition, she didn't even remember driving home.

Inside, she took off her coat and went to the piano. She fingered the ivories and sat down. She played a scale then started Vivaldi's "Winter." Ten bars into the score, she froze. Angry she pounded on the keys, the cacophony such an awful noise the birds started squawking. Sobbing, she lay her arms on the keyboard and lay her head on top of them.

Minutes later, her tears spent, she sat up, wiped the tears away and started thinking about her future. If her career was over, what was there to keep her in New York?

Nothing. Absolutely nothing. Other than the Maestro, David, Mike, and a few other orchestra members, she had no close friends. She was always practicing at the music hall or traveling. As a result, she hadn't had time to make more friends.

The birds ruffled their feathers and talked to each other. Looking about the room, Charlene found herself getting up, then going through the different rooms until she ended up in her bedroom. Her hand slid around the footpost of her bed.

She was home. This was where her father had lived, her grandfather and grandmother. She had roots here.

Why not Willow Junction? She liked it here, liked the community, the hominess. She like working at the orchard.

But, the orchard couldn't support her and Logan both right now. She'd have to do something else, but what?

Plus, she had already agreed to sell the house to Logan.

She called Henry Norton's office only to learn he wasn't in. An appointment made for first thing the next morning, Charlene's hand remained on the phone. She picked up the receiver.

The next phone call was the hardest. She dialed the Maestro's number.

"It's not good news," she said. "My arm... my career is over."

"I suspected as much from what I heard the doctors not telling you."

"But, you never said anything."

"I was hoping for the best. I hated seeing you disappointed before they knew for sure."

She didn't know what to say.

"What are you going to do now?" he asked.

"I have to sell the condo. Without an income—"

"Let me do that for you. In fact, I think I know someone who wants it. I'm going to miss you not being in the city, Charlene. I expect you to come visit and often. You're always welcome to stay here with me when you're in town. You're family."

"Thank you, Maestro. You don't know how much that means to me."

They talked a few minutes more, the Maestro telling her he'd coordinate with Mike and they'd get her belongings packed and shipped as soon as possible.

Catching up on other news, mostly about other members of the symphony, they finally said goodbye with a promise to talk often. Hanging up the phone, she let the tears flow.

She had just turned the last page of the sheet music of what had been her life.

Wiping the tears away, she took a deep breath and dialed Mike's number. *So, this is what starting a new life looks like.*

* * * * *

First thing the next morning, Charlene set out for Marshall and Henry Norton's office.

"The only way the agreement can be nullified is if Logan agrees to it," Henry said, after she'd been escorted into his office and she had explained her situation, that she was staying in Willow Junction.

"That won't happen," she said. "We're at odds right now."

"I'm sorry to hear that. Any chance things will improve?"

"I doubt it."

"And the orchard?"

"We're still partners, but for the most part but I'm leaving its operation to Logan. He knows what he's doing. I'm even considering selling it to him at the end of the year. It'd probably be best for everyone."

"That's too bad."

"Henry, can you please tell me why Charlie made us partners?"

"In light of what you've just told me, I don't suppose it matters one way or another. Charlie's plans, it seems, have failed."

"And they were?"

"To get you and Logan together."

"As partners."

"Romantically."

Charlene blinked.

"He felt the two of you just needed the opportunity to be together, so he provided it. Like I said before, I tried talking him out of it. He was insistent that the two of you were perfect together."

They were or had been. For a while. Charlene sighed.

Minutes later, she was on the sidewalk contemplating what to do next. A sign in the yard next door caught her eye.

She couldn't or wouldn't go to Logan and ask if she could have her house back. She'd made a deal, and she wasn't going to back out. Going through the door of the realtor's office, she hoped she'd find her solution here.

* * * * *

Late that afternoon, Charlene was back home. Inside, she kicked off her shoes. Her feet hurt. It'd been worth it though. To her delight, she and Mrs. Green, the realtor who offered to help her, had scoured the area, and finally found a house down the road that would meet Charlene's needs. Located two miles from the orchard, Charlene had the choice of renting or purchasing.

The realtor admitted that she'd not been in the house since the last renters had left and was dismayed to find the house so rundown, needing significant repairs before it could be rented again. She explained that the owner lived in Florida now and that she was the owner's manager for the house.

When Charlene told Mrs. Green that she wanted to rent but wouldn't be able to do so until March, the realtor assured her that was okay. It would give her and the owner time to make a plan and replace the broken windows, get the furnace fixed, repaint the rooms, and have the house properly cleaned. She told Charlene that she felt the owner would be agreeable to the terms.

Charlene had just sat down when she heard someone knocking on the door. It was Josie.

"Are you ready?"

"Oh, my word. I forgot all about the co-op." Just for a second, she contemplated telling Josie she couldn't go. With Logan there, it would to be uncomfortable and there'd be curious glances if anyone caught on that something was out of sync. But then, she reconsidered.

She had as much right to be there as he did. Technically, she was now a citizen of Willow Junction. She had no intention of staying home and cowering in the corners. "Let me get my shoes," she said.

Since she and Josie were the first to arrive, they went ahead and made sandwiches. John Martin was the next one to arrive, and on his heels the others filed in, too. By the time she was finished in the kitchen and went to the table to join everyone, Charlene noticed with dismay that the last empty seat was next to Logan.

Unwilling to sit there and not talk to him, she decided to meet the problem head on. She sat next to him and spoke quietly so the others couldn't hear. "Why are you avoiding me, Logan?"

"I'm not. You're the one who rejected me."

Charlene stared at her plate. She hadn't rejected him. Only his proposal for now. He had left before she could explain. He sat next to her like a stoic rock. She wanted him to understand. "You know," she began, "there was a time you told me I was as stubborn as Charlie. I'm not the only one holding sheet music to that tune. Logan, I—"

"Don't. I don't want to hear it. I knew better than to get involved with you, but I did. You're a famous pianist for crying out loud. I don't stand a chance next to your career. It was great while it lasted, Charlene, but it's over now. Just leave it."

Logan grabbed his plate, scraped back his chair, and left the table abruptly. Everyone in the room watched him leave. Everyone but her. She picked up a potato chip and stuck it in her mouth. She wanted to choke on it. She bit into it wondering if she'd be able to swallow.

Thankfully, everyone went back to their food and conversation. Throughout the evening she stayed in her own corner of the kitchen sorting sugars and flour, glad for the job, glad her hands were busy. She only wished her mind could be as busy, as well.

* * * * *

Thanksgiving passed quietly for Charlene. Arrangements to rent the house down the road were finalized, giving her a year to make up her mind if she wanted to buy it. With the sale of her condo, she'd be able to.

As she ate her frozen TV turkey dinner, Charlene wondered if Logan and Brian were eating a traditional turkey dinner. She'd stopped going to the salesroom every day ever since the storm. Business had dropped considerably because of colder weather and

Josie said she could easily handle it all by herself. It was best this way, Charlene decided, staying out of his way.

Obviously, Logan was feeling rejected, feeling she had dumped him. Just like Beth. The only trouble was, she wasn't Beth. She had wanted to work out a future together. Maybe they couldn't have gotten married right away what with her tours, but in a year or so they could have.

But now...

Everything had changed. There'd be no tours, but she hadn't any opportunity to tell Logan that.

Charlene dropped her fork. She had no appetite.

Cleaning up the kitchen, Charlene went to work on refinishing a table. Part of her new plan was to open an antique shop. She needed to get the merchandise ready. As she applied the stripper, she grinned thinking how easy it had been to come up with a job.

She'd sell the orchard to Logan, and operate a small store in the downstairs of her new house, living on the top floor. She planned to teach piano after school, too. Good piano teachers were hard to find and even if she couldn't play at length, she could easily teach. At least this way, music wouldn't be entirely gone from her life. She could still play for herself for entertainment, just not for long strenuous lengths of time.

All in all, she expected to finally settle down and create some real roots of her own. Even though she would no longer own any of the family property, she'd be living in the same community. That was what was important. Logan would be an excellent caretaker for Gramps' house and land. She had no regrets whatsoever.

She sighed. Well, only one. She wished she and Logan could have remained friends. Maybe in time it would happen.

* * * * *

The day after Thanksgiving, Josie called her.

"Charlene, how could we have been so stupid?"

"I don't understand."

"Christmas. Everyone goes shopping for Christmas the day after Thanksgiving. I can't tell you how many people have been here today. What are we going to do?"

Charlene thought for a moment. "Why not call our ladies and ask them if they can bring in more stuff—Christmas stuff, you know, angels, Santas, wreaths, bells, candles, that kind of thing and in a couple weeks, we'll hold a Christmas Open House. This will give shoppers something new. By then, maybe they will be tired of malls."

"Sounds good to me. Want me to tell Logan what we're doing?"

"Sure. Go ahead." Charlene knew Josie was being tactful, knowing Logan had been avoiding her.

"Will you be coming back to work in the mornings?"

Charlene wanted to say no, but then considered how unfair it was to Josie. "Sure, I'll be there on Monday."

* * * * *

The next day, Saturday, it snowed.

Brian visited as usual. Hannah was back with her baby,

watching Brian during the day. Totally oblivious to the problems of the two adults, Brian chatted about Hannah's baby and other things of interest to him. Charlene was just grateful that Logan hadn't restricted Brian from visiting her.

"Look what I found," she said, pulling her hands from around behind her back. She held up a pair of ice skates she knew would fit him. "I found these up in the attic. I had them sharpened for you."

"Oh, boy!" Brian exclaimed. "Can I try them right now."

"Not really. There's not enough ice, but I imagine in another couple weeks that won't be a problem."

They spent the afternoon making bird feeders out of milk cartons and throwing nuts to the squirrels.

The following day, Sunday, there was enough snow that they were able to make a snowman nearly as tall as Charlene.

That night, Josie had called her telling her not to come in. The snow had hampered the women from bringing in their merchandise. While Charlene didn't like hearing that sales were down, she was glad for more time to spend refinishing some furniture to sell.

Two more days passed with it snowing continuously.

Now, she and Brian were tramping through the snow, their feet sinking until the tops of their boots nearly disappeared, pulling sleds behind them.

"I was out walking the other day," she told Brian, "and I came across this great hill. Wait till you see it."

Brian pointed out the squirrels that were busy looking for

long ago buried nuts, and Charlene pointed out the birds. She and Brian chattered about everything and nothing until finally they arrived at the hill.

Standing at the top of the hill, Brian surveyed it.

"Is it too steep?" she asked, sensing a reluctance to slide from him.

"No."

"So, who's first?"

"I am!" Brian said, jumping on his sled.

"Do you know how to steer?"

"Yes."

"Let me go down with you this first time so you can show me how you steer."

"Then I can go by myself?"

"Yes, provided you can steer."

"Okay." Their first ride down the hill was uneventful. Ahead was a huge tree, smack in the middle of the slope, but down at the extreme bottom of the hill. Fortunately, they hadn't gotten anywhere near it. They had lots of room before reaching that far, and if they did, they could go around it on either side.

At the top of the hill again, she lined him up, then gave him a small push. He flew down the hill in a straight line again, stopping well before the tree.

Countless times they walked up the hill and slid back down, sometimes together, sometimes separately. The more they slid down the hill, the slicker it became, and Charlene noticed they were starting to come close to the tree.

"Time to go, Brian."

"Ohhhh. Just one more? Pleeeeaaaase?"

Charlene smiled. "Okay. Just one."

Clapping her mittens together to warm her hands, she watched as Brian trudged up the hill, losing his footing now and then, but bounding back up and continuing uphill.

At the bottom of the hill, she waited for him, leaning against the tree, out of harm's way. The last time she'd come down the hill, she'd finally made it past the tree, but had given it wide berth and was confident Brian would too.

"Are you ready?" Brian yelled down at her.

"Ready!"

She watched him push off, then laughed seeing the snow blow up in his face. He lost his footing, then had one foot back in place, but not the other. As he got closer to the bottom of the hill, she saw him struggle to get his foot back into proper position. He wasn't looking at where he was going, and he was heading right for her. And the tree.

Just then, she saw a figure at the top of the hill. It was Logan. "Brian!"

Charlene placed herself between the tree and Brian and his runaway sled. She saw the look of surprise and then fear on the boy's face.

She braced herself, hoping to grab the sled or him from it. One way or another, he wouldn't get past her.

Instead, he ran straight into her and the momentum threw her backward. She heard a snap and then pain as the sled and Brian pinned her to the tree.

Logan ran down the hill, his feet sliding, unable to take his gaze off the pair at the bottom of the hill.

Brian got off the sled and stood.

"Are you all right, son?" Logan shouted, as he slid to a stop, checking Brian first.

"Yeah, Dad. I'm okay. Charlene stopped me."

"You were gone so long. I thought I told you this hill was off limits." He turned to her and knelt down. "Are you okay, Charlene?"

Brian looked at the ground. "I'm sorry."

Charlene grimaced and sat up. Her left arm hurt. "Logan. I had no idea this hill was off limits."

"Brian knew," Logan said, "And, I'd bet he didn't want you to know. Isn't that right, Son?"

Brian nodded, tears forming in his eyes.

Charlene put weight on both her arms to help her get to her feet, but her left arm felt funny and gave way. Sweat beaded on her upper lip and she felt a trickle of perspiration slide down between her breasts as she braced herself and tried to push off the ground with her right hand.

"Charlene?"

She blinked several times, refocusing her eyes. Her arm throbbed and she longed to hold it to her side. But, as long as Logan stood there looking down at her, she wouldn't give him the satisfaction. "Never mind. We're fine. I'm fine. Just fine. Go find someone else to worry about."

Logan sighed and ran a hand through his hair. "You're right. I'm sorry. I was just so scared, seeing Brian racing for the tree like that." He reached for her.

Charlene gasped when he wrapped his fingers around her left arm. Logan's gaze flew to hers, his look was one of surprise, then anxious concern.

Dots clouded her vision. She couldn't think. She could feel herself tilting to the ground. Why did Logan sound so far away?

Chapter 12

Charlene woke up, confused. It was dark. She was in bed, but it wasn't her own.

A soft knock at the door captured her attention.

Josie poked her head into the room. "Good, you're awake. Finally." She came into the room.

"Where am I?"

"In the hospital. Do you remember what happened?"

"I think so."

"You and Brian were sledding—"

"And, I had a confrontation with a tree. How did I get here?"

"Logan brought you to the emergency room. They had to perform surgery on your arm. You broke it in two places this time. They had to insert a pin. You broke a couple fingers too."

"If the last accident hadn't ruined my career, this one sure did."

Wide-eyed, Josie's mouth dropped. "You mean, you won't

be able to play anymore? What are you going to do?"

"Move on. Find a new career. Where's Logan now?"

"I don't know. He spent all night here with you. I've never seen him look so frightened or pale as he did. Except for you. Pale that is. You still look too white to me. How do you feel?"

"Woozy."

"How does the arm feel?"

"Numb. Any idea how long I'll be here?"

"Just a couple days according to what Logan said."

"How's Brian?"

"Worried about you. In fact, he's down in the waiting room. He has permission to see you, but I wanted to make sure you were awake first. I'll go get him."

When Josie left, Charlene wondered why Logan wasn't here, too. Obviously, he didn't want to see her.

The door opened and Brian peeked into the room. He looked around, as if he wasn't sure he was in the right place. Then, he spotted her.

She smiled. "Hi, Brian."

He grinned and ran to her bedside. "Charlene! You're all right."

"Sure. Didn't you think I was?"

"Dad told me you were okay, but I was so scared."

"How is your dad?"

"Grumpy."

She smiled, and glanced at Josie. Josie just shrugged her shoulders.

Brian held out an envelope. "This is for you."

"Everyone heard what happened to you," Josie said. Someone brought a card to the orchard and all morning people came by, signing it." Josie helped Brian open it for her.

Tears formed in Charlene's eyes when she read the card and saw all the signatures.

Lights in the hall flashed.

Josie pulled on Brian. "Visiting hours are over, short stuff."

"Don't worry about Stan and Ollie. I'm taking care of them," Brian said.

"And don't worry about the Christmas sale," Josie added. "I've already had five people volunteer to take your place. Just get well." Josie gave her a hug as best she could.

As the door closed behind them, Charlene sighed. It had been great seeing them, but it'd been tiring, too. Closing her eyes, she wondered when she'd see Logan.

* * * * *

She woke up seeing Jim Davis leaving the room. She frowned trying to remember. What was he doing here? She closed her eyes.

* * * * *

She next remembered waking up to a nurse checking her vitals. Seeing Charlene eyes were open, the nurse commented about the large pile of cards on the night stand. Charlene closed her eyes again, thinking that was Jim's doing.

* * * * *

She'd been home just a couple days now. She had learned

from Josie that Logan had slept in a chair next to her bed that first night. She had never seen him, just Jim delivering the cards. Logan never came to see her.

In another week, they'd be holding their Christmas Open House in the salesroom. She'd have a few pieces of furniture she could display and sell along with a few antique kitchen appliances and glassware from Gramps' kitchen.

As a welcome home present, Brian had given her a drawing of Cat. He helped her frame it in one of the frames Logan had given her. Now it hung in the front parlor.

Charlene sat in front of the fireplace, an afghan tucked around her legs, a novel in her lap, unopened and unread. She stared at Brian's rendition of Cat.

Though he still stopped every afternoon, his visits were short. He wasn't supposed to be bothering her, he told her. Instructions from Logan, apparently.

She sighed. She'd miss their daily visits once she moved, but she would make a point to spend time with him.

Brian had confided that he'd gone sledding once since the accident, but it hadn't been nearly as much fun as when she had been with him. A baby hill instead, he claimed.

She replayed that day in her mind. The most vivid memory was Logan's expression when he realized she was hurt. He'd been stunned thinking that he'd hurt her physically. Yet, he was hurting her worse by staying away. Why was he avoiding her?

Someone knocked on the front door. Two men, with the rest of her New York belongings from the condo, and they wanted to know where she wanted the stuff unloaded.

She showed them where to stack it in the front room opposite the parlor, where it'd be out of the way for now.

She watched as they brought in her furniture and boxes of dishes, clothing, and everything else she owned. If only she was moving next week instead of in three months.

For now, she'd just have to settle for packing up the rest of Gramps' stuff that she would be selling in her new shop and getting this house ready for Logan and Brian.

* * * * *

Logan slowed his pickup to let the big van pull out of Charlene's driveway before he pulled in. Nervous, he turned off the engine, got out, and walked up the porch.

He knocked, then saw her peek through the window. Cold, he cupped his hands and blew into them. He'd forgotten his gloves, and it had started snowing again.

When she didn't open the door right away, he wondered if she didn't want to see him. If she didn't, he couldn't blame her, not after the way he'd been acting. Finally, he saw the doorknob turning. She opened the door.

Peeking through the window, Charlene had been surprised to see Logan standing at the door. He looked so good, even if his shoulders were hunched from the cold. He cupped his hands to his mouth and blew. Her heart raced as she reached for the doorknob.

"Hi," he said.

She stood gazing at him.

"May I come in?"

She stepped aside. He smelled just like the outdoors... and like chocolate. She doubted she'd ever be able to smell chocolate again without thinking of him. She couldn't stop looking at him. Blue eyes stared back at her, his cheeks red from the outdoors, strands of blond hair drifting downward onto his forehead.

"Take off your coat," she said.

She watched him remove his coat and hang it on the hall tree.

"Looks like you're getting ready to move to New York. Not that I blame you. It's probably a lot safer than Willow Junction these days. I saw the van outside. Did the antique dealer pick up the furniture?"

Looking around the parlor, Charlene guessed he came to the conclusion she was moving to New York because the room was so empty. While the two men were here, she had them move some furniture to the back so she could work on it. The two birds, their cages, and piano were more prominent now in the front room.

"I'm not going back to New York," she finally told him.

"You're not? But the boxes... where are you going?"

"Down the road."

"I don't understand."

"I've known for a while that my career is over. I just couldn't accept it, didn't want to admit it to myself. My arm won't ever be the same again. There's nothing in New York for me anymore. Not really. My family's history is here in Willow Junction. I've found something here that I want to keep. A sense of belonging. I never felt that in New York. I've rented a house down the road."

"No, you're not. This was you family's home, still is as far as I'm concerned no matter what arrangement we made."

"But Logan—"

"No buts. Do you think I could live here knowing you were down the road somewhere? I couldn't. Either you live here or it'll stand empty."

She swallowed hard. She didn't know what to say. "Thank you," she said softly. She'd get to keep her heritage after all.

"What will you do about a job?" he asked. "The orchard may not be able to support itself next year, not after this loss."

"I'm going to teach piano and classes in furniture restoration, plus open my own little shop. It was going to be downstairs in the new house, but here, I suppose the front room would work."

"I had an idea that we could should plant Indian corn and pumpkins at the orchard, getting the kids to come out at Halloween."

"That's a good idea. I like it." Charlene went to the roll-top desk and pulled something from one of the slots. She handed it to Logan.

He unfolded it. It was a check. He looked at her, a puzzled expression on his face. "What's this?"

"Proceeds from the sale of my condo after my bills were paid. Now that I won't have to buy another house, I want to invest the proceeds into the orchard."

He held it out to her. "No. I can't accept this. This is your money."

"It's to buy the equipment we need. All of it. Used, of course."

"You can't just give that money to the business."

"Then it's a business loan, an investment for my future."

"Would you be interested in making another investment," he asked.

"I'm all tapped out, but go ahead. I'm listening."

"Be my partner."

"I already am, Logan. And, I plan to be a silent partner until the year is up, then I'm selling my half to you. You've got everything under control. You don't need me. It can be a land contract, with payments."

"I need you more than you could know. First of all, I need you as a working partner. Josie needs a vacation, lunch, and someone to talk with. At least, that's what she keeps telling me. She's so busy now she doesn't have time to gossip on the phone. She didn't want me to tell you because she didn't want you worrying about the orchard.

"Second, sales have never been higher, despite the loss we suffered from the storm. The damage wasn't near as bad as I first thought. The bulk of the added income came from the country shop. But, we'll know better next spring. Third, what will I do with that empty room if you don't come to work on a regular basis?"

"What empty room?"

"The expansion. Those last plans that were delivered, the ones you accepted and gave to me... they were plans for the salesroom—to knock out the bad wall and expand the salesroom so we could sell more crafts. You and Josie proved a country theme is an asset and what with our history and background, it'd be a natural. You also proved there is a market for that kind of thing and while we're at it, why not add your antiques to it. It's better for us to be diversified."

"Only if the orchard takes a commission and I'm selling on consignment."

"Okay, but only if you take a salary for the hours you work." No, I—"

"No buts" he said. "And fourth—"

"There's a fourth?"

"None of this will be worthwhile unless you agree to put me out of my misery. After Beth walked out on me, I was afraid to love again. So, I told myself I wouldn't love anyone. Little did I realize I couldn't help but love other people; you pointed that out to me.

"Brian wants you to join our family. Become my partner for life. Say you'll marry me. I love you, Charlene Walker." He tugged her into his arms and gave her a long, heart-stopping kiss.

Breathless when they finally parted, she whispered, "And, I love you. Yes, I'll marry you."

"Honey, you've made me the happiest man in the world."

"Marry me," Ollie chirped.

"Kiss me, baby," Stan answered.

—0—

DIANA STOUT

Acknowledgments

My sincere thanks to Ruth Stout and an extra special thank you to Anne Stone.

About the author

Diana Stout, MFA, Ph.D. is an award-winning screenwriter, author, and former English professor whose writing led her into academic teaching. Her students would say, "She smiles when she talks about writing." Published in multiple genres, she enjoys helping other writers learn the craft.

When not writing, she enjoys reading, watching movies, the rain and birds at her feeders, gardening, jigsaw puzzles, and visiting with family and friends.

To learn more about Diana, you can visit the following:

Sharpened Pencils Productions: sharpenedpencilsproductions.com
Facebook author page: www.facebook.com/writerDianaStout
Twitter: twitter.com/ScreenWryter13
Pinterest: www.pinterest.com/drdianastout
Goodreads: goodreads.com/user/show/43124185-diana-stout

Blogs
Only for the Brave – a writer's life: http://wryterinwonderland.com
Behind the Scenes – business about writing: http://dianastout.net
Into the Core – experiences as an intuitive: http://dianastout.com

Writing a Review

Did you know that reviews are important for other readers and for authors?

Only through reviews can authors understand what their readers want. Writers need your honest thoughts about their stories. And readers rely on reviews when determining whether to read a story or not.

Did you like this book?

Please help other readers discover if this book is one they might like to read.

Did you know that you can use the same review on other websites where this book is sold or downloaded?

Yes, you can! Feel free to repost your review anywhere you find the book or novella being sold or where reviews are posted.

A review doesn't have to be long.

Should you decide to leave a review on Amazon or Goodreads, thank you for your feedback!

Made in the USA
Lexington, KY
31 October 2019